I had just gone under when I heard the noise that woke me.

Though not immediately sure what exactly the noise was, I quickly decided it was somebody stopping in his tracks, perhaps surprised to see a man and woman sharing a bed in this house. We'd left the hall light on, because in tight spots, where you don't want to go deep, it can be helpful in bringing you immediately awake, which is what it did now, for both of us.

And the figure in the doorway, just a silhouette with hallway light framing him, found himself facing two wide awake people sitting up in bed and training weapons on him...

QUARRY'S RETURN

by **Max Allan Collins**

A HARD CASE CRIME NOVEL

A HARD CASE CRIME BOOK
(HCC-165)
First Hard Case Crime edition: November 2024

Published by

Titan Books
A division of Titan Publishing Group Ltd
144 Southwark Street
London SE1 0UP

in collaboration with Winterfall LLC

Print edition ISBN 978-1-80336-876-4
E-book ISBN 978-1-80336-877-1

Design direction by Max Phillips
www.signalfoundry.com

Typeset by Swordsmith Productions

The name "Hard Case Crime" and the Hard Case Crime logo are trademarks of Winterfall LLC. Hard Case Crime books are selected and edited by Charles Ardai.

Printed and bound by CPI (UK) Ltd, Croydon CR0 4YY

Visit us on the web at www.HardCaseCrime.com

For my granddaughter
LUCY COLLINS
but not for a while…

*"Murder, like talent, seems
occasionally to run in families."*
GEORGE HENRY LEWES

*"It takes a powerful motivation to lead to murder.
That's why people don't usually
murder comparative strangers."*
ERLE STANLEY GARDNER

ONE

You would think a retired hitman would know better than to answer a knock at the door, on a snowy winter's evening, without bringing his gun along.

Let's stop right there. I rarely if ever heard anybody in the killing game use the word "hitman," except in an arch manner. They would just refer to themselves as professionals, and the prior job as a piece of work they'd done. Anyway, I had no reason to think at this late stage of my existence that I might be the target of a contract killing myself.

While we're at it, nobody in the business called the target a "target," either. A "mark" maybe. But more often the "subject." To be fair, we did use "hit" sometimes. It's just that a lot of nonsense has been written about my former profession and I like to keep the record straight.

In my slight defense, I had only done contract killing for five years or so, a long time ago. Right after I got home from Vietnam and nobody except a pompous, well-dressed son of a bitch called the Broker (long dead now) had any work to offer me of any kind. I had auto mechanic skills but even the repair garages were fussy, after I kicked the jack out on a sportscar my wife's boyfriend was working under. No, I did no time for killing the prick—I was back from the war and traumatized and they decided not to throw my ass in prison. Not that they had any work for me, either.

At least in stir I could have made license plates.

Now when I say I only worked as a contract assassin for five years or so—as if that takes the sting out—I am omitting that I wound up with what I called the Broker's list. You'd call it a database today, but we didn't have home computers yet, and it was actually a little metal recipe box with names and phone numbers and other info, which I used for a decade or so to track my fellow contract workers to their next jobs. I would then approach their marks and offer my services.

That included taking out the usual two-person team sent in to do the job, which of course I'd already surveilled, and tracking down who had taken out the hit, and removing that individual. The Broker had acted not only as agent for these professionals, but as buffer for his clients, meaning who had sent them was rarely known to the assassins. So determining who wanted the subject dead, and removing that party, was the tricky part, and I'd charged big for that.

Still, if you think about it, I'd only been in the killing business for fifteen or twenty years or so, and that was decades ago. Since then I'd run a couple of legit businesses, and had been married twice, first to a sweet simple soul who'd become collateral damage when my past caught up to me. Just last year my second wife, as smart as her predecessor wasn't, fell prey to Covid. Janet had been a librarian who'd inherited a lot of money when I figured out why I'd been lured out of my previous retirement to kill her, and decided to wed her instead. Required removing a few assholes from the planet to do so, but nothing in life is free.

Anyway, generally I understand that my personal history is a rocky one, and you don't answer the door without brushing back the curtain facing the deck, and checking to see who the hell had come calling.

Wasn't like I didn't take precautions. In the years since my killing people for Uncle Sam, and then in civilian life killing for profit, I'd had the past come hit me in the face now and then like a loose board. So I had guns salted all around the great room (as my late wife called it) of the two-story cabin-in-name-only that came along with Sylvan Lodge, where I'd been a sort of caretaker till Janet, my wife, inherited money and we bought the place.

It was a seasonal business, shuttered right now, so having somebody knock at my door would generally get my attention. I would reach my hand down between the cushions of whatever chair or couch I might be lounging in, in front of the field-stone fireplace over which my flat-screen TV perched, and be ready to rumble.

Of course I'm not as ready to rumble as I once was. But there were worse-in-condition seventy-one-year-olds around. I was slim and I worked out three days a week and swam daily in the fitness center across from the main resort building, where even the convenience store and its gas station were closed for the season.

True, I'd had double bypass surgery a few years ago, but I had lost my paunch after Janet died and my five-ten was strictly muscle and tendons and veins and the kind of steel-gray hair that had waitresses still giving me a come hither look even at this late date. Of course the Brainerd bunch all knew I had money, so that was probably it.

The knock was insistent but not obnoxious and I went right over to it, without checking out the glass of the double doors to see what car might be pulled in past the deck, without looking through the damn peek hole, not even digging one of those cushion-tucked handguns out. What an idiot.

In my pitiful defense, I have to say my daughter Susan had been staying with me over Christmas. I'd even put a tree up, an artificial fir from Wal-Mart—Sylvan Lake was ringed with the real thing and I was not about to buy one—and draped white lights were still twinkling even now. Past the double doors that overlooked the deck, the plastic pine stood in the corner like a naughty child.

Susan had just left in her silver Cadillac CT5, after sharing an awkward hug—neither of us comfortable with that kind of thing—and she'd been gone only fifteen minutes, give or take, and I figured she'd forgotten something and come back for it.

Only it wasn't Susan.

The man on my doorstep, lost in a black topcoat with elaborate lapels, was rather small, perhaps five-seven, and he had the professional look not of an assassin but of perhaps an accountant. His hair was black mingled minorly with white, his eyes were blue and rather large behind wire-frame glasses, and he had the kind of trim mustache you used to see little guys wear trying to look like Clark Gable.

Of course he was maybe thirty-five and likely never heard of Gable.

"Mr. Keller?" he said, in a pleasant tenor. He had a toothy smile that went well with it.

Jack Keller was how they knew me around here. I'd had a lot of names, none my own, going all the way back to when I signed on with the Broker.

"I'm Jack Keller," I said, friendly, keeping all the tightness inside, watching his hands, which were in black leather gloves, folded in front of him.

"I apologize for just dropping by," he said. "I did leave several messages on your machine."

"Oh. You're Mr. Duval. I did get your messages. You didn't say what you wanted, so frankly I didn't bother responding."

"Well, I can understand that." He shivered. "Quite a cold snap, this evening. Any chance I could step inside?"

If this was a threat, if this small, pleasant individual was here to kill me, better to handle this now. Better to deal with him on my terms. On my turf.

"Sure," I said, backing up, gesturing toward the two-story open-beamed great room, adjacent to a small modern kitchen tucked under the partial second floor. "Let me take your coat."

"No, that's all right," he said. "I won't take up that much of your time."

Moving with confidence, but not quickly enough to cause alarm, he headed toward the nearest chair, a comfy leather number with cushions. And a .22 revolver stuffed safely away between the latter, which of course he did not know about. A glass-topped coffee table was in front of him and he caught the edge of the fire I had going, which cast some orange and blue reflections on him.

He got out of his gloves and tucked them in his pockets. I was a coiled spring waiting for him to come back with a gun. All right, a senior-citizen coiled spring....

But his hands were empty, and he used them to quickly un-button his coat, which he shrugged off and put behind him like a cocoon he'd crawled out of. He flickered with fire, some of it bouncing off the coffee-table glass. He lifted his right hand toward his jacket, also black, though his tie added some Christmas color, red-and-white slanting stripes like a candy cane that melted.

He was a festive undertaker in all that black.

Of course, I was in black, too. Black sweats, black running shoes. Nothing the color of a candy cane on me, though. I was standing there taking in my guest and his careful moves. At the moment that right hand near where his white shirt and black jacket met was frozen in mid-air, as if it hadn't recovered from the chill yet.

"I'd like to interview you, Mr. Keller," he said. "For the *Star Tribune*? Might I record us on my phone?"

I was ready for him, so I said, "Why not?"

He got his phone out, slowly, and tapped its face a few places, then set it on the coffee table. Nothing suspicious about it, except the care he took making it look like nothing suspicious.

My arms were at my side. Folding them would have been dangerous. Foolhardy, even. And I'd already been foolhardy enough.

"Why in the world," I said pleasantly, serving up a smile, "would you want to interview me? I manage a tourist lodge. That's the start and finish of it."

"I've spoken to some folks here in Sylvan Lake," he said, and he meant the nearby little town of Sylvan Lake, not underwater, "and you have a sterling reputation."

Nobody had ever referred to my reputation as sterling before, not even in this straight life.

But I said, "Well, that's good to hear."

And that did sound like the kind of artificial tripe somebody writing for a newspaper might come up with.

"If I could make a suggestion," I said casually, as I edged past the coffee table and came around and sat in the comfy chair adjacent (but not quite next) to him, "you'd do me a lot more good if your paper ran something after the season starts. My activities when we're shut down could be summed up in a few lines."

Duval turned in his chair so he could face me. Leaned forward, folded his arms and let them hang between his legs. "Meaning no offense whatsoever, Mr. Keller, you are not the subject of the piece."

"Oh?"

"No. It's your daughter."

Not what I wanted to hear.

I gestured easily toward the lake. "Well, you just missed her. She spent Christmas with me. She's on her way home now."

"I'm aware of that," he said, and laughed a little as if that were amusing. "My editor has already arranged for a stringer… that's a journalist there in the Quad Cities, where your daughter lives…to do an interview with her."

"I know what a stringer is," I said, perhaps just a little testy.

"My editor wants pictures of her at home," he explained, "in her work area. And I understand the house she's in was designed by Frank Lloyd Wright, so we'll get some interesting pictures, I'm sure."

"Actually it's not by Wright. It's a knockoff of one of his houses, but it is pretty cool. You'll get some nice pictures. You've set this up with her already?"

He nodded, his smile settling on one side of his face, the skimpy mustache coming along for the ride. "We have. Or I should say my editor has."

"She didn't mention it."

He frowned a little, mildly surprised, or pretending to be. "Would she generally share that kind of thing with you? Publicity of that sort?"

"Why wouldn't she?"

"Why would she?" This was affable enough, followed by a shrug. "Mr. Keller, you should be a proud father. Your daughter is a very successful person. A writer of some renown."

I was already on alert, but now the hairs on the back of my neck had come to attention.

"I *am* proud of her," I said. "But I'm not much interested in true-crime stuff."

"Surely she's spoken to you about her book *Sniper* being optioned by the movies."

"She may have mentioned that in passing."

"It's really a masterpiece of its kind." His left hand painted a picture in the air. "*Sniper—The Killer Who Came Home.* A normal Midwestern boy is twisted into a killing machine for his country. I understand Matt Damon is interested."

"I wouldn't know."

He sighed, leaned forward even more. "Let me be frank."

He could be Frank or Oscar or Harry, as far as I was concerned.

But I said, "Please."

"Our research indicates you and your daughter had no known contact prior to a little over a year ago. Were you estranged? If I might ask."

"You might ask, but I'm not inclined to answer. You're wading into rather personal territory."

He raised his palms in surrender. "Fair enough." He leaned back in the chair. "Are you by chance aware of an article that appeared in a publication called *Paperback Quarterly*?"

"No."

And I wasn't. I had never heard of it.

His shrug was more elaborate this time. "Well, why should you be? It's a minor publication. For fans of pulp fiction. Afficionados of literary junk food."

"I like westerns myself."

"I prefer cinema. Foreign cinema, actually."

"I was including spaghetti westerns."

He laughed. "Ah! Sergio Leone! The best. I knew we'd find some common ground."

I was very close to killing him. My hand had slipped down between the cushions and was gripping a .22 semi-automatic. It wasn't really what he had said, or what he was saying: it was that he was morphing into another person. He was letting the mask slip, whether on purpose or not I couldn't tell you.

He raised a hand and waved it a bit, as if indicating he was moving on to another topic. Or in this case, back to one.

"Now, this publication for fans of old paperbacks. One of them did an interesting article about a series of books about a character called Quarry."

Oh, he was going to die, all right. Unless I did.

"In these novels, Quarry was a sniper in Vietnam who came home and found himself cuckolded by his young wife. He killed the wife's lover...dropped a car on him, actually...and went to work for someone called the Broker. A sort of agent for hitmen."

Again, we rarely used that word.

"Now, the names in Susan Breedlove's book, *Sniper*, were different. Quarry was something else, the Broker was something else. But this little article, this obscure little article, paralleled the books in that cheap series of novels that appeared way back in the mid-1970s, with your daughter's true-crime account. An eerie coincidence, don't you think?"

The .22 auto came out a little slow, caught by the leather of the cushion, and my slight fumble gave him time to rock back in the chair and take it with him, and after he and it went down, he had something to hide behind.

But he didn't come up and return fire.

Of course, he didn't know a gun was tucked away between the cushions of the very chair he was hiding behind. So what his thinking was, I couldn't tell you. Every pro in the killing business has his own way of doing things. Some specialize in vehicular homicide. Others use their hands. Some plant explosives. To each his own.

But what was this guy's jam, as the kids say?

"I researched you, Keller," he said. From behind the chair, on its side now, he had a muffled sound. "You're a rich man. You can buy me off. For the right price I'll give you my broker's name, and you can work your way back to whoever wants you dead. I don't know who that is, of course. Things haven't changed that much in the trade since you were in it. There's still that buffer. Interested?"

"I might be," I said.

I was on my feet, facing the chair on its side. The coffee table was off to my right slightly and the fire was cracking and crackling and throwing shadows and making shapes.

He crawled out and, with his hands high, stood.

Here's where I went wrong. I should have shot him immediately. In a way, I got greedy—not the money kind of greedy, the greedy for information variety.

Some kind of rig on his wrist fed his right hand a knife, a stiletto switchblade that he clicked open and hurled at me and it caught my sleeve and some skin too but it was mostly the surprise that sent the .22 flying from my hand and onto the field-stone hearth.

So *that* was his fucking jam.

A blade man, one of the sickest kind of fucks in a business littered with sick fucks. And he had another damn stiletto switchblade, probably more than just one, in the pocket of his suit jacket, and that came out and clicked, too, as he charged at me with it in his fist, raised to stab.

We didn't have much distance between us, but I jockeyed around to put the coffee table in the way of his assault, and he had to circle it before he could dive at me and I grabbed the cell phone he'd put on the glassed top and flung it, hard, and it caught him in the chest, knocking him back, back-pedaling into that chair on its side he'd been hiding behind.

But he still had the knife, and even as he bumped hard against that sideways chair he had the presence of mind and the dexterity to flip positions of the weapon, to go from a fist that was ready to stab downward to an upward blade held by tight curled fingers and a guiding thumb.

That gave me pause and I eyed the .22 on the hearth and went for it.

He was fast. No question. He was right there to kick the .22 away. He had the knife in hand, his fist still holding it in that upward manner, where he could guide it with surgical skill. In an eye blink he retrieved the .22 and was pointing it at me with his left hand while the blade in his right scolded me like a sharp finger.

"You're him, aren't you?" he said.

His voice was different now. The mustache—Christ, it was fake, it was hanging from his lip like a half-picked scab! And the hair was askew—a wig! This bastard really went all the way. Disguises, stiletto switchblades up the wazoo—I didn't know whether to admire him or fit him for a straitjacket.

"Sure," I said, looking up as the fire did its demonic dance on the hovering figure. "I'm him. But who's him?"

"You're *Quarry!* You're fucking Quarry!"

"Well, you win the Powerball, dipshit."

I kicked him in his balls, only they weren't so powerful, because the pain doubled him over and he stumbled backward and I tackled him.

I'll be honest with you. Like I said, I am in good shape for seventy-one. And this guy was smaller than me. But he was also younger, by a quarter century at least. That he had a gun in one hand and a knife in the other made wrestling with him tricky. He caught me with a few shallow stabs in the back and batted me a couple times with that .22, and then he squirmed out of my grasp and was standing over me with the automatic pointing down at me, the small black barrel looking bigger than anything I'd ever seen. Like it could swallow me.

Forever.

The gunshot that rang out in the high-beamed room made

me shudder, like a kid fooled by a jump scare in a horror movie.

But the bullet flew over my head and thunked into a wall or somewhere, and my faux-journalist guest straightened, as if something above him had caught his attention. His candy-cane tie ribboned red, while the fireplace continued its devilish dervish. He joined in, dancing on dead feet, well just shuffling really, before tumbling onto his back as the twinkling white lights of the Christmas tree in the corner welcomed him to oblivion.

With him on his back, someone else was revealed, someone who had come in the door unheard, a beautiful woman of indeterminate age, in a white fur-collared parka over a black jumpsuit, her hair black now (it had been blonde), her high-cheekboned face with its Asian-cast features shockingly familiar.

I was still on the floor, leaning on my elbows.

"Lu," I said. "Aren't you dead?"

Her voice was familiar, too; throaty, sultry.

"Only on paper," she said.

TWO

I either fell asleep or passed out and, when I woke up what turned out to be half an hour later, my first thought was that I'd imagined or dreamed Lu being there.

I had been told by what I thought was a reliable source that the lovely female assassin was dead, that she'd been killed in a robbery at the antiques shop in Minneapolis that had been a profitable front for her other business. That business was being a regional broker in the killing game, a position she'd risen to over the years.

We'd first met years ago when I used the Broker's list to follow her to her next gig. She'd been Glenna Cole then. I had disrupted that job, but along the way we'd had a sort of affair and I managed not to have to kill her. She turned up a few decades ago and bailed me out of a situation not unlike this one: saving my life when I was under the gun.

The two times were similar enough that I might well have dreamed her presence before blacking out. But when I came around—positioned face down on a couch near the twinkling white lights of the Christmas tree—with some pillows under me and my head lower than my heart, which was good procedure for dealing with the kind of wounds I'd suffered—she was kneeling nearby, snapping off some latex gloves that might have been mine. Or maybe she traveled with them, should something come up.

Like it had here.

"Welcome to the land of the living," she said huskily.

She was fucking beautiful and not just because she'd saved my life. With those Asian eyes, the almond cast with gold-flecked blue orbs, combined with the new hairstyle, jet black in a Bettie Page cut, she could have walked out of the old Russ Meyer flick, *Faster, Pussycat! Kill! Kill!* If you haven't seen it, I can wait while you go off and correct that lapse. Google Tura Satana while you're at it.

"What are *you* doing in it?" I said, craning my head toward her. "The land of living, I mean."

"I paid a pretty penny to die and disappear," she said, the eyes widening just a trifle. "You should try it. Might prevent people from coming around trying to kill you."

I flicked a look toward my bare back, not seeing much of anything. I seemed to still be in the black sweatpants. "How bad?"

I remembered my visitor, in our wrestling match, stabbing me a couple of times with one of his stilettos.

"Not bad," she said. "Two were a little deep, two others glorified cuts. I applied pressure for fifteen minutes on both deeper ones. I irrigated the wounds with tap water. Using Betadine, which you had in your medicine cabinet, or rubbing alcohol or peroxide, might have done more harm than good."

"I notice you don't use peroxide anymore."

"Never did. I always used Nice 'n Easy."

"You…you always were a nice and easy gal."

"Be quiet. Rest."

Something was going on, on my bare back. "What's that you're doing?"

"Just daubing on some bacitracin. Then I'm going to put band-aids on both lacerations. You want any pain killer? Any morphine around somewhere?"

"I don't do opioids. I'm a very clean-cut boy. Get me three or four of those 500-milligram Tylenol. They're on the kitchen counter with some other meds."

"You old people and your meds."

That was a joke and the slight curve at one corner of her lovely mouth said so. She was probably not far from my age, though she looked like a well-preserved forty-something. Probably worked out. Not a vegan, because they tend to pork up on pasta, and even in retirement she would need her protein.

She got me my Tylenol and a cup of water. Still on my stomach, I managed to take the pills and wash them down.

"My caller," I said. "Dead, I assume."

Her nod made the black scythe blades of her hair swing. "Yes. There's enough blood on the floor that we'll need luminol in clean-up."

"I don't…don't keep luminol around. But there's hydrogen bleach under the kitchen counter. That…that'll do the trick."

"It will." She patted my butt. "You grab some sleep. I'll wrap up our friend. Where do you keep your roll of plastic?"

Not, *Do you keep a roll of plastic*—where.

"Front closet," I said, "toward the back."

She nodded and I nodded off.

Back in the latex gloves, Lu was just finishing the round-and-round duct-taping of the cylindrical package of plastic that contained the late Duval or whoever the fuck he was. Duct tape is something every household needs to have on hand.

She had moved the coffee table and my chair back somewhat to make room for the process. I noticed that the black topcoat my caller had worn was draped over my chair, which she'd righted. Kneeling now, she noticed me noticing that.

I sat up with a little difficulty, but sat up nonetheless. My black sweatshirt was folded neatly on the floor nearby. I started to reach for it and she said scoldingly, "Don't get ambitious. Just sit there and get your shit together."

"Okay," I said. A woman wrapping up a corpse in plastic sheeting and duct tape is not to be argued with. I nodded toward the enshrouded remains. "Why didn't you include the topcoat in that package?"

She ripped off a piece of duct tape; it was like a robot farting. "It's a nice coat. I like it. Nothing identifying, no labels or laundry mark. Tried it on and it fits fine. Any objections?"

"No. Seems like the least of the indignities our guest is facing."

Her shrug was dismissive. "He died quick. That's the best people in our line can hope for." She finished her work with that last silver strip, then got to her feet and said, looking a little embarrassed, "I, uh…he had two hundred bucks and change in his billfold. I'm keeping it for expenses. I drove from Billings."

"Montana?"

"It's the only Billings I know."

"That's ten hours easy."

One skinny eyebrow went up. "It's eleven and not easy at all. Required more coffee than any human being should endure."

"You should try Diet Coke."

"No. That shit can kill you." She looked down at her handiwork; it was reflecting the fireplace glow on one side and the twinkling Christmas lights on the other, like an effect in a science-fiction movie. "I put his billfold back. He had three fake I.D.'s and enough random business cards to form a chamber of commerce. Nothing worth keeping. Nothing we could trace. Any thoughts about what we should do with him?"

I didn't feel half bad. The Tylenol was doing its stuff. "The lake isn't frozen yet, but I don't like shitting where I eat."

"Who does? Any water-filled gravel pits handy?"

"Quite a few, actually, around Brainerd." I'd made use of one or two before. "That's the best idea. Closer to home than I'd like, but not in my back yard."

She strode over to me, tall and curvy in the black jumpsuit, snapping off the latex gloves again.

"You up to a nature excursion?" she asked. "After dark's the best time to do something like this, and that would be right now. Or we could wait an hour or—"

"No. I'm fine. I had a hell of a nurse."

That got a tiny pleased smile out of her. "We far from where you have in mind?"

"No. It's a place the locals call Quarry Park."

The small smile blossomed into a grin—rare for her. Plenty of sly smiles from this one, but a grin? Alert the media.

She said, "You wouldn't kid a girl would you?"

I retrieved my sweatshirt. "Not one who just wrapped a corpse in plastic, I wouldn't."

Soon we were on our way to Quarry Park, an abandoned site that had been owned and operated by the Brainerd Crushed Stone Company. By the late twentieth century, when the firm went broke, they'd quarried out a thousand-foot-long, hundred-foot-high cliff of coarse-grained, dark-colored, intrusive igneous rock called black gabbo, an obelisk that loomed like a rough-hewn vertical tombstone above an unsafe body of water. Many a swimmer had drowned there, thanks to underwater growth that caught them by the ankles like the Creature from the Black Lagoon. Quarry Park was scenic but it could be nasty.

Lu was behind the wheel of her black Lexus while I played navigator filling her in on where we were going down this ribbon of country road. Trees on either side of us edged plenty of sky. The night was cold and clear, a near full moon like a prison searchlight guiding the way.

"Since they shut down," I was telling her, "the quarry has been an area where locals can walk their dogs and hike and picnic. There's a nice view of the nearest lake to take in, too, if you climb to the top."

"Summer mostly?"

An Oldies station was playing on the radio, softly. Right now they were spinning the Classics IV doing "Spooky." I swear.

"Summer," I confirmed. "But also, during the winter, it's a training ground for recreational rappelers and university students in climbing programs."

Lu threw me a sharp look. "Not at *this* time of night."

"Not this time of night, no."

She let some air out; stayed focused on the road. We had it pretty much to ourselves.

"So," she said. "Enough with the tour guide crap. Tell me— do you know what this is about?"

"The dead guy in your trunk?"

Eyes on the road. "The dead guy in my trunk. The professional someone sent to kill you."

"Maybe I do. How about you, Lu—do you think *you* know?"

The slightest smile. "I asked you first."

I tasted my tongue; one serving was plenty. "I don't know specifically. But I…I think it has something to do with my daughter."

Bobby Darin was doing "Eighteen Yellow Roses."

Those almond eyes were on me now and widening. "You have a daughter?"

"Right now I do. But for how long?"

I filled her in quickly about Susan's success as an author of true-crime bestsellers—my daughter was famous enough that

Lu, though not a reader, had heard of her—and that Susan had written about my years working with the Broker in a book called *Sniper*.

"I saw that in an airport!" Lu said, shocked. "That's about you?"

"Yes. But she didn't use my real name. Or anybody's real name, except a few victims."

Her eyebrows were up, what there was of them—they were plucked into expressive lines. "Am...am *I* in it?"

"A bit, but just a mysterious figure. A lovely creature of the night."

"What am I, Dracula's daughter?"

"You tell me," I said. "There's more."

The eyebrows were still up. "Isn't that enough?"

"I've written some books myself."

"*What?*"

"Novels. That got published. Not under my name, and not using real names or places. Kind of...based on my experiences."

"Oh, wonderful."

The Four Seasons sang "Big Girls Don't Cry" softly in the background.

"Don't worry—I never made it into the airports. And nobody ever connected the real-life dots till Susan started digging in. But she found enough out about those early years to write *Sniper*, and was moving into my later, uh, experiences...when she came around to see me."

Lu was studying me like a biologist who'd come across a brand-new germ. "And that was the first you knew Susan was your daughter."

I shook my head. "Actually, I didn't know at first. Kind of figured it out a while later. I met her mother on a job in Iowa back in the early '70s."

"By met her mother," she said dryly, "you mean knocked her mother up."

Paul McCartney was singing "Till There Was You" with the Beatles.

I shifted in my seat. "That's an impolite way to put it, but… yeah. Peg was a beauty, Susan's mother. A *Playboy* bunny, back in the day."

"You always did have refined tastes."

Lu didn't ask me anything else for a while. She seemed kind of irritated with me. What, jealous? We hadn't even met at the time.

Before long she had pulled into a flat area where snow-dusted gravel was being overtaken by scrubby weeds. Several mounds of crushed rock had been left behind when quarry operations ceased, gray hills washed ivory in the moonlight. The face of the black cliff above the murky water went straight up, but the backside was a steep slope that didn't encourage climbing, recreational or otherwise.

We got out. Lu was in the dead man's black topcoat and I was in my fur-collared black bomber jacket. We were like messengers of death who'd brought a duct-taped package to deliver to nobody.

The silence was, as they say, deafening. Not a bird nor an insect had a thing to say. The chill breeze was just enough to ruffle the dead leaves of trees and the piny branches of evergreens made a mute audience on the other side of the water, which had an old swimming hole look. That aspect of it had lured any number of kids and teens to their premature demise.

Lu and I walked the area to make sure we were alone, which seemed to be the case. I had my nine millimeter Browning, an old friend, in my jacket pocket; and she was armed, I knew. We got the plastic-wrapped mummy from her trunk and I carried it on one side, gripping it around the shoulders, with Lu on the other, gripping it by the calves. We walked it over to the cliff, unlikely pallbearers, and started up the slope in back.

Unbidden, Lu began to explain her presence. "A few days ago I ran into somebody I knew. Someone in the killing game, who I represented in my broker days."

"Wasn't he surprised to find you alive?"

"He was happy to, but it's not like he was looking for me, at least as far as I can tell. It was just happenstance. Chance meeting in a restaurant bar. Seems we both lived in Billings. I explained my situation, that I had spent a small fortune buying my death and a new life. He pledged discretion. And he was interested because that sounded like an option he wouldn't mind taking himself."

"An incentive not to expose you."

"Yes. Exactly."

Our shoes were crunching rock beneath us.

"Anyway," she continued, "we always got along. We were friendly. It felt like I could trust him."

"Dangerous."

"I know. But these things happen. I wasn't living in a hole. Dead or not, I was existing right out in the open, just on new ground. Come on, Quarry—you've been exposed a couple of times. The only place you can really hide is under six feet of dirt."

"True."

"So we had dinner together and started to talk and he was a drinker, you know? He mentioned that he was about to leave town on a job. Then he laughed and said his mark was someone who used to be in the business. Somebody with a big rep. He'd been told to be on his toes. I didn't ask who he was talking about, but he blurts it—'Quarry,' he says. 'Ever run across him?'"

I stumbled in my hauling. "Really. And what did you say?"

"That I never had. Never heard of this Quarry character. What made *him* special? He said, 'For the life of me, I couldn't tell you.' He said you were just an old fart now. In your seventies. Retired for years. You wouldn't even see it coming."

"This guy you ran into," I said as we lugged him along, "is he our friend here? Who's about to go for a swim?"

"Yep."

We were there, at the apex. Both of us, for our age, were in good shape. In her case, maybe great shape. But we were both a little out of breath. We set the package down and put our hands on our hips and breathed hard till we didn't have to.

Finally she asked, "Shall we?"

"We didn't come here for the exercise."

"I didn't weight him down, you know."

I shrugged. "He'll stay under till the gases kick in, then float to the top. No getting around that, unless we want to spend more time on this than it deserves."

We lifted him, with her at his waist and me at his ankles and we did the heave-ho bit. He sailed out nicely, and I would swear he hung in mid-air for a split second before his lower weight took him down and he went in feet first. The water hardly splashed; it was more like the gravel pit swallowed him. If I'd been scoring, I'd rate him a goddamn 10.

In the Lexus, I snapped my seat belt in place and said, "You didn't have to come all this way to warn me. Why wait till he was in my lap before interceding?"

"Your phone number isn't exactly listed," she said, and started the car up. She didn't continue explaining till we'd pulled out of the makeshift park. "After he and I parted ways, I jumped in my car and followed him. Figured he'd go to a hotel or motel or whatever."

"He didn't?"

"No. Despite the fact that he was half in the bag, he headed out of town on 94. Drove five hours to Bismarck, which is about halfway. I had a getaway bag in my trunk, money and clothes and such, so I just, you know, hung in there."

"Followed him to my place."

"When I saw the lakefront home, I figured that was you. You always live that way. Right on a lake, where you can defend a frontal attack or take a swim, whichever you might be in the mood for."

That made me smile a little. "And you looked for a way in but didn't find one."

"No. No unlocked back door or windows that could slide up. Finally I used a hairpin to unlock on the deck doors. Didn't have my lockpicks along. Took my time, made sure someone was talking when I did my thing. I could have interrupted sooner, but I was listening to the conversation, trying to get a fix on what was going on."

"Well, he was there to kill me, is what was going on."

"No, but why? I'm not sure I agree with your assessment of the situation, that this had something to do with your daughter."

"Not knowing the why of it didn't stop you from shooting that prick and helping me dump him in that gravel pit."

"No it didn't. But what's your take, exactly?"

I sighed. "My daughter must be delving into some unsolved crime and has stirred up the wrong kind of interest from the right kind of miscreant. And she doesn't do just any kind of crime—it's all serial killings and husbands killing rich wives and—"

"Snipers who come home with PTSD?"

"Very funny." I shook a fist. "I need to warn her—she should be home by now—and I'll go help her figure out what snake she stirred, poking around."

Lu was nodding slowly, the arcs of black hair swinging gently.

"That's certainly a possibility. But I heard what your late visitor had to say—he knew who you were and was trying to extort money out of you. There are plenty of people out there who even at this late date would like to see you dead."

I locked my eyes with hers. "When Susan and I first got together, somebody had targeted me. Somebody from my past, and I went wading through the best suspects and took out the ones that needed it."

"No possibility somebody else could be out there."

"Well…sure. Sure there could."

We had pulled in at the lane that took us past the sleeping lodge at left and, as we drove a ways, the resort's guest cabins nestled in the trees at right, and then at left was my two-story cabin-ish dwelling. Lu pulled into the blacktop area in front of my deck, stopped the motor and turned to me.

"What next?"

I gave her a grateful smile. "Next I thank you for saving my life, not to mention getting rid of the residue. I can do any remaining clean-up myself—I've used bleach before. You head back to Billings. Maybe I'll look you up someday."

"No. I'm sticking."

I frowned. "What do you mean?"

She jerked a thumb at the impressive shelf of her bosom. "I'm the one who shot that son of a bitch. I'm your accomplice in getting rid of the body. I am in this from now till we find a safe exit. You have your cell phone on you?"

"I do."

"Try your daughter. Like you said, she should be back in the Quad Cities by now."

I was shaking my head. "Lu…Jesus Christ. You've done enough. You've done plenty."

"No. I'm *in* this. Call her."

I got the cell out and tried Susan's cell first and it went to voicemail. I tried her landline. Got the machine.

On the latter, I left this message: "This is your father. Go to a hotel. You'll hear from me soon."

I clicked off and turned to Lu.

"She isn't back yet," I said. "She will be."

But I didn't sound sure of that. Which I wasn't. Might have been intercepted long before.

Lu touched my nearest shoulder. "Let's go in and get fresh dressings on those knife wounds. Pack a small bag in case we're gone a while. Get yourself a can of Diet Coke and we can stop on the way for gas and some fast food."

"On the way where?"

"To the Quad Cities. To your daughter."

THREE

I packed a small suitcase with several changes of clothes, including a sports coat, my zippered toiletry kit, and my nine millimeter Browning semi-automatic handgun. I'd had the nine mil for decades, going all the way back to Broker days, and it was as close to my favorite weapon as a fucking killing tool could be. Additionally I packed the noise suppressor that fitted it, and several spare clips. The gun nuts insist you call them magazines, but we called them clips in country, which is to say Vietnam, and that's good enough for me.

I left a voicemail message for my maintenance guy, José, the only other year-round employee of Sylvan Lodge, who worked only two days a week off-season. I let him know I'd be away for a while, confident he'd dependably look after the place.

Lu was already ready, but I could see she was dragging. While I packed, she drifted off in a sitting position on the couch where she'd tended to my wounds. After all, despite her time-less Dragon Lady looks, she had to be damn near my age. I was powered by adrenaline for survival and fear for my daughter's safety; but Lu had involved herself out of sheer curiosity and maybe a touch of caring about what happened to me, an old friend. Crashing would be inevitable.

I sat next to her and she woke with a start. Her head had been back and now it jerked forward. She had her .38 Police Positive snub-nose revolver in her lap; the gun came up.

"Easy," I said. "Don't kill me. I'm too young to die."

"You're too old to be alive."

"Listen. Honey."

She frowned. "Did you just call me 'honey'?"

"I did. Would you prefer 'sweetheart'?"

She was stern. "No. I prefer 'Lu.'"

"Okay, Lu. I calculate it's been fourteen hours, at least, since you left Billings. And who knows how long you were up before that. How did you manage it?"

She shrugged. "Uppers."

"I take it they've worn off."

"They have. I shouldn't take any more for a while. You're going to have to do the driving."

I gave her a reassuring smile. "I'd already arrived at that. I'm alert and I've done the Sylvan Lake to Davenport run any number of times. You got the car keys off our dead visitor, right?"

"I did. It's a key fob. We'll need to find his car and dump it."

"Right. Then let's get started. Let me grab a Diet Coke first."

"Your version of uppers."

She wasn't wrong. I grabbed a chilled six-pack and locked up and we made our exit.

The late Duval's car was all alone in the parking lot behind the main lodge building, a pearl-white Honda Accord that seemed to glow in the moonlight. For now, Lu was behind the wheel of the Lexus. She pulled alongside the Honda and I got out. I used the fob and searched the interior, glove box and under the seat and everywhere, and checked the trunk, too. Showroom clean. I got behind the wheel. I'd already told her to follow me.

She did so, and twenty miles outside of Sylvan Lake, I pulled off on a country road and, after five miles or so, swung into a farmer's access mini-lane. With a rag I'd brought along for this purpose, I wiped the steering wheel and anything else I touched, or even might have touched, both inside and out. Lu was in the graveled country road with the motor going, the eyes of the headlights watching me; her almond-shaped orbs were doing the same.

I came around to take over the driving. She had the window down and looked up at me curiously, like I was a carhop and she was having trouble deciding what to order.

She asked, "A little close to home, isn't it?"

"That plastic package we deposited at ye ol' swimmin' hole will bob up soon enough. This area's been a dumping ground for the aftermath of Minnesota and Illinois mob disputes for decades. Won't lead the local cops anywhere but to the wrong assumptions."

Then I was behind the wheel. I drove down to the next access inlet, pulled in and backed out, and returned to Highway 94, by which time Lu had already put her seat back and gone soundly to sleep. She snored a little. Not enough to drown out the Oldies station on the radio. In fact, it might have seemed cute, only nothing about Lu was cute. Beautiful, yes; frightening, certainly. But not cute.

The five-hundred-mile or so trip would easily take seven hours. And I didn't dare speed and risk being stopped, no matter how concerned I was about Susan's well-being, because I had a nine millimeter, noise suppressor and spare clips in my suitcase. And Lu was armed with the .38, which she'd used to stop my caller from killing me. The gun was in a pocket of the black topcoat bequeathed her by the corpse.

Starting out the trip by killing a highway patrol cop would be counterproductive. With these dashboard cameras they had these days, our vehicle would be promptly made and suddenly Lu and I would be a modern-day Bonnie and Clyde.

I had better things to do than shoot it out with cops.

I had a daughter to save.

❖

Last week, a few days before Christmas, I'd taken Susan out for a nice meal. On the main drag connecting Brainerd and adjacent Baxter, the Black Bear restaurant was a big sprawling log building that looked like a cabin got out of hand. Our table and chairs were rough-hewn wood, and a massive stone fireplace and log walls provided the requisite coziness.

My daughter was a petite, curvy little number with a pretty oval face framed by short naturally blonde hair, her eyes big and blue. She was in her early forties but looked at least ten years younger. She wore a cream-colored turtleneck and blue jeans and high heel boots, and decades ago she would have been my type. Her mother had been.

We talked about nothing of import or even interest throughout my walleye and her salmon, but then we shared a piece of cheesecake with two forks creating an intimacy that finally broke through the awkwardness. Several glasses of wine also helped.

Look, meeting your daughter for the first time when you're about seventy and she is in her early forties—a daughter you only recently learned you had—means there's going to be discomfort. Our interaction was aided and abetted by a similar sense of humor, however, and when somebody from my past had been trying to kill me last year, she had saved my life once and I had saved her life once and that had warmed up the relationship.

But still.

"Do you have any contact," I asked, "with your ex-husband?"

She shook her head and her hair seemed to shiver at the thought. "None. With no kids, what's the point? He was an embezzling, cheating prick, and who needs reunions?"

I had a bite of cheesecake. "When was your breakup?"

"Ten years ago, give or take." She studied a bite of cheesecake on her fork, before committing to it. "We *did* try to make a go of it. I didn't turn him in for stealing from me...I made good money on my books, particularly the Unabomber one, and could afford to look the other way, once...plus he swore he'd be faithful to me from then on out."

"But he wasn't?"

"I'm not sure. What went wrong was..." She took the bite, seemed to consider it and the rest of her response. "I'm not sure it's dinner-table conversation."

"I'm your fucking father. Spill."

She laughed a little. "You talk like a paperback tough guy, sometimes. Did you make any money on those books?"

"Don't change the subject. What went wrong with your marriage? I think any man lucky enough to have you should learn to behave himself."

"Spoken like a proud papa."

We were past wine and she was on to coffee. I was having hot tea.

"I told you, Jack..." She called me "Jack," as that was my first name around here and she wasn't comfortable with any form of address in the vein of dad or father. "...how I can't have kids. That you aren't in any danger of running into any grand-kiddies out there in the wild."

"Yes."

"Well, that was how I learned I couldn't have children. We took all the usual tests, and...turned out there's something wrong with me inside."

Me too.

She was tearing up. I hadn't seen that before, from this cool cookie, and it shook me some. I thought about it a while and, and after she dabbed her eyes with a napkin, finally reached out and touched her hand.

"The past," I said, "is never worth crying over."

"Is that a quote? Who said that?"

"I did. Just now."

She laughed a little. "You and your positive attitude. I used a quote from you in *Sniper*, you may recall—not *quite* so positive."

"I don't recall."

"'Though I'd learned in Nam to accept life and death as meaningless, I'd also learned the importance of survival.'"

I grunted a non-laugh. "That doesn't make sense."

"Well, you said it. Or wrote it."

We finished our dessert.

She was having one last cup of coffee when she looked at me, deadly serious. "Something I want to ask you."

"Why not? We're well past secrets, you and I."

She leaned in and spoke very quietly. Very.

"Should I feel guilty?"

"About what?"

A whisper: "The two men I killed."

I almost laughed, which would not have been an appropriate response.

Instead I said, softly, "One asshole was about to kill me, and the other had you tied in a fucking chair and would've killed us both. *Of course* you shouldn't feel guilty."

Susan sighed. Relief was in there, but some other things, too.

She said, "Yet I've been feeling guilty about *not* feeling guilty. Is that silly? Stupid?"

"Yes. Yes."

I paid the check and walked her out into a chilly evening where meager snowflakes were threatening to turn into something. She hooked her arm in mine, and that was nice.

Part of me regretted what she'd had to endure because of me, last year, when my past came calling.

Part of me was fucking proud of her.

After all, guilt is just a coward's conscience.

And you can quote me.

Christmas Eve I made supper for us. I am no master chef and a short-order cook in the worst greasy spoon would rate me pitiful. Most of the time I take my meals at the lodge restaurant, a perk of being the owner. But off-season I survive on a handful of things I know how to put together in my own little kitchen, like spaghetti with bottled Ragu, boxed jambalaya, and skillet-prepared cheeseburgers. Also various frozen items, like Stouffer's Chipped Beef on Toast, aka Shit-on-a-Shingle as we Marines called it, for which (master of cookery that I am) I substitute biscuits. Since it was red, spaghetti seemed like the Christmas Eve ticket.

After that, Susan and I sat in the great room, a fire going in the fieldstone fireplace, cups of hot chocolate in hand. We were wearing ugly Christmas sweaters I'd bought for the occasion. I had pulled the couch around to face the Christmas tree I'd bought her, because I knew she was sentimental about this time of year. I didn't know why.

So I asked.

"Then Christmas was something special at your house?"

"It was," she said. "I had no brothers or sisters, and most of Mom's family was either deceased or lived far out of state. That made it just the two of us. She spoiled me rotten. I received just about every toy the Sears catalog had to offer. And as a teenager I got clothes and LPs and books, books, books."

"My Yuletides were pretty damn bare-bone."

"Really?"

"Yeah. My dad was a typical male who didn't know from gifts. My mom was dead and my stepmother had zero time for me."

"Evil stepmother, huh?"

My eyebrows went up. "Oh yeah. Everything but the magic mirror and poisoned apples."

That made her laugh. "Do you ever wonder if…no, that's not fair."

"If I'd wound up with your mother? What my life would've been like? Well, I tried."

The blue eyes got bigger. "Really?"

I sighed. "She made me tell her who I was. *What* I was. If I'd lied to her, maybe I could have pulled it off. But when I told her the truth about some things that had been going on in her little town, since I arrived. That I was…was…"

"Quarry?"

I nodded. "I might have had a different life, yes. You might have, too." My sigh was as wistful as I get. "She was a real catch, your mother."

"Sweet and kind."

"I was thinking of that *Playboy* Bunny nude layout, and the successful restaurant and bar she ran for all those years. A babe with money ain't all bad, y'know."

She slapped my arm. It was a rare show of direct affection. She almost made me spill my hot chocolate.

"Was she the…you know…the love of your life, Jack?"

She was one of them. How many times had I been on the job, on some nasty-ass job, when a good woman reared her head and gave me the opportunity to change my ways and return to a normal life? My parents hadn't been perfect, but I had a decent life growing up, a normal life, until Uncle Sugar traded me three grand a year for it without asking my opinion.

And Joni was supposed to be waiting for me when I got home from overseas, but I came in on that mechanic working on her back end like she was another car, and I didn't kill him right away, I stewed about it and confronted him in his driveway a day later and kicked out the fucking jack and the back of that car crushed him. Then came the Broker, and five years of murder for hire, until...

Margaret Baker.

Peg.

Something had come alive in me, thanks to her. Something I thought was dead. Something that could have given me a clean start. Of course I had to kill the Broker first....

I'd gone home and waited a little while and then I called her. Called Peg hoping a new life might begin.

What was it I did, she'd wanted to know. Was it...kill people? I'd said nothing, but she'd said goodbye.

There had been others who'd held out that kind of hope.

A smart, uneducated girl in Biloxi. That giving coed in a theater balcony in Memphis. That curvy Black campaign worker in Missouri. That knowing barmaid, also in Missouri. That mob guy's naive daughter in Iowa City. That sad sweet trailer-park mom in Illinois.

Then Linda.

And Janet.

But first there had been Peg.

Under the tree, no presents awaited. We had both said there'd be no gift exchange. That would be silly in our odd situation. Just getting together would be plenty. Would be more than enough.

But suddenly she said, embarrassed, "I *did* get you something."

"We weren't going to..."

"It's not exactly a gift. I wrapped it, but...it's just something I want you to have. I could give it to you any ol' time. But why not now?"

"Okay. But first, well, I uh...so did I."

She frowned, confused. "So you did what?"

"Got you something. Probably not exactly the ideal gift, I admit. It's kind of like giving a woman a vacuum cleaner or a MixMaster for her birthday. Okay if I grab it?"

"Sure." She seemed interested. Intrigued.

I went to where I'd stowed it. I hadn't wrapped it. I had stuck a red bow on it that I bought at the Dollar Store in Brainerd.

I handed her the present and sat back down.

It was a shoe box and she asked me if it was shoes.

"Not shoes," I said. "Open it."

From within tissue paper that she peeled away, the present emerged: a Browning Hi-Power nine millimeter handgun with walnut grips.

"It's a big weapon for a woman," I admitted, "but it's the kind of armament that has served me well. I can exchange it for something else if you like."

"No," she said, wide-eyed, holding the Browning in a hand that looked small or maybe the gun just looked big. "I love it. Is it...loaded?"

"No. What kind of jackass gives his daughter a loaded nine millimeter handgun for Christmas? I have some clips for you."

She hefted it, getting used to the feel. "What's your, uh, thinking here, Jack?"

I shifted on my couch cushion. "I'm afraid, last year, I brought a lot of trouble to your doorstep. For better or worse, some people seem to know about our...connection. You need protection and this is a start."

"Thank you," she said, it sounded genuine. Her eyes were on me and her face was alive with the reflection of the shimmering white lights from the tree. They might have been stars or snowflakes or tears.

She got up and went back to the guest bedroom where she'd
been staying and returned with a box about the size of a ream
of paper; the thing was heavy and its wrapping had *Toy Story*
characters on it in a Christmas theme.

"That's meant to be kind of a joke," she said with an awkward
smile. "What it's wrapped in."

"It's fun," I conceded. "Those movies are scary and that's
good for kids. They need to know life is scary."

"Open it."

I unwrapped the box.

Lifted the lid.

Inside was a fat stack of typing-type paper and on the top
was a card-sized envelope with "Jack" on it. I opened it and the
Christmas card within was very generic—*To My Father* on the
front, and *Your Loving Daughter* inside.

She was looking at it over my shoulder and said, sheepish,
"That was the least lovey-dovey I could find. Sorry."

"No, it's great." But also within the envelope was a flash drive.
"What's this?"

"Look at the title page," she said, nodding toward the contents of the box.

It said:

SNIPER 2: YOU CAN'T GO HOME AGAIN
A NON-FICTION NOVEL
BY
SUSAN BREEDLOVE

"This is the sequel?" I asked.

She nodded. "It's everything else about you, from the 'list'
years through what happened to your first wife through our,
uh, fun and games last year."

"I already wrote my version of that. I sent it to you."

"I know, I know. And it's been published and well-received by its audience."

"Not a big audience like yours. No airports."

She shrugged. "For now, this will have to do."

"What do you mean?"

Susan patted the manuscript like a baby's ass. "I finished that book and it's all in there, and it's the best thing I've ever done. Because it has me in it. I don't mean as a character, or anyway not just because I'm one of the main characters. But because it has my heart and my soul in it, and don't look at me like that."

"When is this coming out?"

"Not for a long while."

"What?"

"I didn't pre-sell it. Didn't sell it at all. Didn't take an advance. I'm not publishing it right now."

"Then…when?"

She shrugged. "When you're gone, maybe. I'll probably live longer than you, don't you think?"

There was my girl. Fuck sentiment.

I asked, "What's the idea?"

She pointed at the manuscript in the box. "The idea is that's the only physical copy, and the flash drive is the backup. I deleted it from my computer. If I find the manuscript in your papers, assuming I don't get hit by a bus before you finally make your exit, I will send it to my publisher. If I don't find it among your things, that's your call. You can burn it right now if you like."

I said again, "What's the idea?"

"I intruded into your life enough," she said. "You wrote about that, in your Quarry persona, and for now that's good enough. Maybe it's good enough, forever. I found what I was looking for. My father."

I didn't know what to say.

Then the silence demanded I fill it.

"Thank you," I said, and added, "darling."

She hugged me, hugged me hard. First time ever.

And maybe the last.

FOUR

By the time we got to the Iowa/Illinois Quad Cities, it was after
one A.M. Lu had slept the entire way, not waking till we were
on Davenport's River Drive, with its impressive view of the
Missis-sippi, the lights of Rock Island just across the way twinkling like low-lying stars. The only people who could afford a residence on this rarefied Q-C stretch, linking Davenport and
Bettendorf, would need money enough for a mansion.

My daughter's place might not have been a mansion exactly,
but it was definitely not chopped liver. A knockoff of a Frank
Lloyd Wright original built around the year of my birth, Susan's
residence was a one-story oddity among the mostly two-story
manses on the bluff facing the river and River Drive. Hers was a
low-slung pagoda affair, its red-brick walls shared with tall windows, some of which were fashioned of glass blocks. Bordering
pines lent the place privacy from neighbors, though this impressive 20th Century Modern house could be glimpsed from River
Drive, like a window on a past predicting a future that never
happened.

The structure came into full view as I tooled Lu's Lexus up
the gently winding red-brick drive. Her appraisal was, for her, a
rave.

"Cool," she said.

The drive ended at a little brick apron by a two-car garage.
The windows of the latter revealed no vehicle at home. The
house itself seemed asleep, those tall narrow windows curtained within and frost-covered without, no lights in back of
them to make them glow. Dark as the house was, it was nicely

illuminated by the full moon. I had my nine mil in hand as I got out of the vehicle and Lu was similarly armed, her .38 Police Positive revolver at the ready. I led the way past snow-flecked shrubbery up an unshoveled walk, noting the lack of footprints. If anybody had stopped by lately, they'd gone in the back way through the kitchen.

Lu still wore the late Duval's black topcoat over her black jumpsuit and boots, and I was in running shoes, jeans and a long-sleeve dark blue sweatshirt under my leather jacket. Nothing suspicious about us except the guns in our gloved hands. Despite the long drive, and Lu getting only a few hours of sleep, we were both alert in the crisply cold air. No snowfall at the moment, but a breeze was moving flakes around, some targeting us.

My daughter and I, after the various troubles we'd navigated last year, had started taking a few precautions, should my past come looking for me again. We each had a key to the other's house; we had shared laptop passwords. Those and a few other minor safety measures we'd followed—nothing elaborate.

Susan had left Sylvan Lake well before Lu and I had, and if she had gone straight home she could theoretically be inside. Not likely, though, because I'd left messages on my daughter's cell as well as her landline's answering machine, leaving instructions to get out and into a hotel till she heard from me. We hadn't mentioned the hotel by name, but we both knew it would be the Concort Inn—another of those minor precautions—and I'd already called to see if she was registered and she wasn't. And there'd been no message from her on my cell about anything.

The chance of my forty-something child being here at home, alive and well, were scant. If she'd made it back, she would have been grabbed or killed. Lu and I hadn't discussed this. We just knew it.

Just as Lu knew to stand to one side of the front door, with her back to the brick wall, while I used the key, prepared to push the door open and quickly plaster myself on the other side of the entry, echoing Lu's position.

This I did, but the door going open prompted no response from within—not from Susan, an unlikelihood anyway, nor from any intruder who might be waiting.

I said, sotto voce, "I'll go in low and to the left. Do the same but go right."

Her nod was slow, the Asian eyes narrow, the .38 barrel up.

I went in fast, and low, and to the left, and Lu followed as instructed. No barrage of gunfire met us, and I quickly reached up and hit the switch just inside the door to reveal a big open space—no entryway—a thirty-foot-square room with, just to my right, walls of glass that had they not been curtained would have provided a magnificent view of the river at night with Rock Island's lights glimmering across the way.

I knew this big room to have been carefully, even meticulously decorated by my daughter, the furnishings strictly genuine collector pieces or high-end reproductions, with framed fine-art modernist prints and a few originals, including a LeRoy Neiman original painting from *Playboy* in its glory days of a lovely platinum blonde Bunny spilling out of her bodice like oversize scoops in a sundae dish.

Peg Baker.

In her prime. Susan's mother and my major missed opportunity. Displayed in a place of honor here in my daughter's home.

Only right now the valuable painting had been yanked from its rightful position and discarded like a used tissue against the upended modern couch, its mustard-color cushions scattered; the couch had been moved off the square throw rug of gold-and-gray geometric squares and dragged back to look beneath it, as if some asshole thought a secret door was waiting under there. Since this place didn't have a basement, that would be a good trick.

The entire room looked like the aftermath of the kind of tornado that usually reserved its Midwestern fury for trailer parks. The slate-gray coffee table was on its side, its top cracked, the David Hockney book that lived on it dumped off. Several squat beige spindly-legged armchairs had been cast aside, their seats checked underneath perhaps, but at any rate transformed from collector's items into kindling.

"Somebody tossed the place," Lu said.

"You think?"

She gave me a sideways look, black arcs of hair swinging. "So I stated the obvious. Sue me. Want me to clear the rest of the house?"

"I doubt anyone's still here," I said, relieved that the Neiman painting of Peg at least didn't look damaged, "but I'll do it. Kitchen's over there, past that louvered divider. Check that, would you?"

That earned a nod.

I went room to room. I knew where the light switches were, so I'd reach my left hand around and illuminate each area before throwing myself in on my belly with my nine mil at the ready. I did this for every room on either side of the hallway and felt like a fool each time; by the end of the process I felt like a fucking fool.

On the other hand, nobody killed me. But then nobody seemed to be in the house, at least not so far. What remained of someone having been here was the results of a search that had turned my daughter's organized, neat-as-a-pin place into a garbage dump.

I joined Lu in the living room. "Whole joint has been trashed."

"You think?"

I deserved that.

"Let's concentrate on her office," I said. "We may come up with something that got overlooked. Something stuck in a book, for example. Something hidden away."

Lu's head bobbed in agreement.

Susan's empty desk, with its drawers pulled out and dumped and gone-through, provided a disturbing presence, as if her ghost—a thought that indicated part of me was assuming her death—were supervising our fruitless search.

And it *was* fruitless. We spent a good hour riffling through Susan's reference volumes, to no avail, and there was no sign of any hard copies of articles from the net. A closet, already gone through ruthlessly, added nothing.

After, we sat at the scaled-down picnic table in the small cypress-dominated kitchen. Lu made coffee, after clearing away some mess—the freezer had been emptied and the contents not returned, just frozen this and that sitting in puddles on a counter—and had found a Coke Zero for me.

"Maybe you shouldn't drink that," she said.

"Oh?"

"You really need some sleep. That's full of caffeine."

Said the woman who had existed on uppers till not long ago.

I popped the pop can. "We're probably heading back anyway." Swigged. "We'll split up the driving."

"No. Take a few sips and let it go at that. You need some sleep." She leaned forward. "There are no signs whatsoever that they took Susan from here."

"How can you tell in this mess?"

One well-sculpted eyebrow rose. "There's a difference when things are knocked over in a struggle. This isn't that—no blood anywhere for one thing. This is the aftermath of a search. It has that feel of things being cast aside once examined."

She wasn't wrong.

I sipped the Coke Zero. "You think she was grabbed up north? Before she even left the Brainerd area?"

Lu nodded and kept nodding a while. "That's my guess. They were prepared to take you on, on that turf, not long after your daughter left. Why would they follow her all the way home before grabbing her? What's the advantage?"

Again, I couldn't disagree.

She went on: "They could do that just as easily without a trip here. Oh, somebody worked this end, all right." With a small smile, she added, "Even my house doesn't get this messy on its own."

I managed a smile in return. "I hardly think you exist in a mess. You're nothing if not tidy."

"Thank you." She had a slurp of coffee; most of the cup remained—she was avoiding caffeine herself, it seemed. "I would suggest you catch a few hours of sleep. I could use a little more sack time myself."

"No! We need to stay at this."

Cool as outdoors, she said, "Stay at what? Stay on it where? Quarry, it's not like you to be emotional, much less irrational."

That felt like a slap, but one I needed. "So what do you see as the next move?"

Her shrug came casual. "Like I said. Sleep. Just a few hours, then head back north."

I sighed. "It *is* possible I might hear, back home, from whoever took her. If it's a kidnapping, after all. They may want a ransom."

But she was shaking her head, swaying those arcs of black again. "Not a ransom, probably. Anyway, not money. Information. I noticed there was no computer in her office. Did she work on a laptop?"

I nodded. "That's the only computer she had, and she took it with her when she traveled. And backed her work up in the cloud."

The almond eyes were thoughtful. "Do you know how to access it?"

"No," I said, and made a face. "Susan and I should have thought of my needing to."

"Not necessarily. We still don't know if this is about you or her."

"Don't we? This place being tossed stem to stern would indicate this is about whatever true-crime case she's working on for her next bestseller."

Lu didn't appear convinced. "But you were the subject of *Sniper*. They could be looking for material related to you and your past."

I stood firm. "I don't think so. They knew where I was. Somebody wanted me out of the picture. They wanted me dead. And it might have happened, too, if the late Duval hadn't interrupted his efforts to try to extort me."

She was nodding again, a slow-motion version now. "So you're convinced this is about whatever Susan was currently researching. What crime or crimes she was digging into, for her next book."

"I have no doubt."

"Did she ever mention what her current project was?"

"No. Only in the most general terms."

Lu's lips smirked and her eyes narrowed. "Come on, Quarry. Be as specific as you can."

"I got the impression it had to do with serial killing. A serial killer, not yet captured, and in the true-crime world that's a golden ticket."

Lu mulled that. "Doesn't make sense. What serial killer hires professional killers like Duval? You're *sure* Susan never indicated she was digging into organized crime in some fashion?"

I shrugged. "No, and I'm not that sure it's a serial killer either. It was more like, 'This next one'll be the biggest thing since Ted Bundy.' "

"Not the biggest thing since John Gotti."

"No." Another sip of Coke Zero. "But I agree with you. A serial killer, a lunatic like that, would do his own dirty work and not hire it done. Would not be connected to the world where you can hire that done—organized crime or big business or spook shit. Really, this is not making sense."

Her sigh stopped just short of a yawn. "Why don't you get some sleep? I could use a few more hours myself. We'll talk about it in the morning and regroup."

I frowned at her. "And just do nothing tonight?"

"What else *can* we do? What else do we *know* to do? We catch a few winks, maybe have some breakfast on the road when we head back north. Talk it out. What say?"

I sighed. Reluctantly, I nodded.

In the guest room, I straightened things up some. This was where I stayed when I visited, so it felt a little like home away from home. The bed was a double one, the walls decorated with Frank Lloyd Wright framed photographs, portraits of the architect and shots of some of the homes and buildings he'd designed. These had been snatched off their wall perches and pitched to the floor, but I hung them back up. I stripped to my shorts and got under the disrupted covers, irritated that the last hands that touched these sheets and blankets had belonged to some interloper.

I put the nine mil under where my head would rest, a good, firm pillow that really did the trick, and anyway I was used to sleeping with a gun under my head at home. I shut off the nightstand lamp and had barely done so when Lu's tall slender shape filled the doorway. Some light in the hall said she was in a skimpy bra and panties. Despite her height, she had an hourglass element. Her breasts were too large for her lanky frame, but nobody's perfect.

She had the .38 in hand.

"Room for one more?" she asked.

"Sure."

Lu came over slowly, slinkily, and slipped under the covers, after tucking her .38 under her pillow. She knew how to get a good night's rest, too.

"No funny business tonight," I said.

"I know." Archly, she added, " 'Not tonight, darling, I have a headache.' Not usually the man's line, but…"

"Hey. We'll get around to it. Just not right now."

"I understand. I don't blame you. But I thought you might like some company, anyway."

She cuddled next to me. I was on my side and facing away, so I guess you'd call it spooning. My dick twitched but neither of us were up for it, though obviously Lu was game. For her, action and danger always had an aphrodisiac effect. Not me, so much.

I was goddamned tired. No question. But I didn't go immediately to sleep. I ran through all the possibilities of what might be going on and what I could reasonably do about it and nothing presented itself. I was glad to have Lu in the game, though, and she was sleeping, snoring her almost-cute snore a little, her arm around my waist, her warmth against me.

I had just gone under when I heard the noise that woke me.

Though not immediately sure what exactly the noise was, I quickly decided it was somebody stopping in his tracks, perhaps surprised to see a man and woman sharing a bed in this house. We'd left the hall light on, because in tight spots, where you don't want to go deep, it can be helpful in bringing you immediately awake, which is what it did now, for both of us.

And the figure in the doorway, just a silhouette with hallway light framing him, found himself facing two wide awake people sitting up in bed and training weapons on him.

Before he could react, those weapons blasted away, the reddish-orange glow of muzzle flash appearing twice, and then the doorway was empty—the invader scurrying away down the hall, something I could hear despite the ringing in my ears from the discharge of two handguns in our small space.

Lu was the first one out into the hall, and I noticed she had a nice tan (vacation? tanning bed?) to contrast with the pink of bra and panties as she scurried out. I followed in my boxers and trailed after her, the interloper heading from the mouth of the hall and cutting left into the big living room.

That would give him ample opportunity to find something to hide behind—we had righted much of the furniture in our search—and that stopped Lu and me in our pursuit. We paused at corridor's end, backs to the pebbled-plaster wall.

We could hear him to our left, moving furniture.

I whispered: "Let's try not to kill him."

He might know something.

"Agreed," she whispered back. "For now."

I got in front of Lu and again sotto voce: "I'll dive straight ahead, you use the wall for cover but see if you can wound him."

As promised, I dove and he was behind the couch, only its rear mustard-colored cushions still on, popping up to fire, a medium-sized guy in a black ski mask and black jeans, and his shot creased my right bicep and my goddamn fingers sprang open as if in surprise and the nine mil fumbled away.

Shit fuck cunt piss hell, getting old was a bitch!

He came charging at me, this would-be ninja in a ski mask, and Lu tried a few shots but he was damn fast and the bullets landed just behind him and thunked into the wall. Then he was looming over me and pointing a weapon down, a .22 automatic from the look of it, and I kicked him in the balls, which seemed to be my go-to martial arts move at this age.

I got up somehow—the meds I'm on make me a little dizzy when I get up too fast—but still I managed to tackle him. We struggled and he was trying to work his .22 into my face and I was trying not to get shot in the eye or anything when I sensed Lu hovering, her .38 pointing down and trying to get a clean shot off that wouldn't kill me or my attacker.

He was squirming and grunting, and I suppose I was, too, but the gun went off, firing just under my right arm and setting my sweatshirt on fire in a patch about the size of a saucer and I got him by the wrist and twisted and the gun went off again, this time putting a red dot in his ski-masked forehead like he'd just arrived from India. I fast-patted the burning fabric till the fire was out just as his eyes got very wide and startled and then empty, and I pushed the corpse off of me. The acrid smell of the scorched fabric clung to my nostrils.

Lu helped me up.

"So much," she said, "for just wounding him."

"Well," I said, pointing to his forehead, "*that's* a wound. A fatal one, but a wound." On the floor behind him, a glop of green and red and gray stuff that had been inside his head lay like a sick animal's feces.

I said to Lu, "See if you know him. Maybe he was one of yours back when you were brokering."

She pulled the ski mask off. His face was wrinkled but not old—kind of a young bulldog. Of course he *was* old—you don't get any older than what he was, a dead body on the floor.

"Nobody I've ever seen," she said. "How bad is your arm?"

"Like they say in the movies—just a flesh wound."

"I bet it hurts worse than in the movies."

"You got that right."

"Come with me," she said, and led me by the hand down the hall into the bathroom, where she cleaned and bandaged what was in fact a minor wound.

"I can't take you anywhere," she said.

"We better check our new friend for I.D."

She sighed. "A waste of time, but why not?"

He had no I.D. on him. Not much of anything, just an extra clip and about a hundred dollars in ones, tens and twenties. We'd keep that. Gas money.

Speaking of which…

"We better head back north," I said. "To my place. Regroup. Rethink."

She glanced down at the dead invader. "What about this piece of shit?"

I said, "We better take him with us. Put him in the trunk till we can find a quiet place to drop him in a ditch by the side of the road."

Annoyed, Lu said, "We need to wrap him in something. I don't need to drive around with this bastard's DNA in my trunk. I assume your daughter doesn't have a roll of plastic handy, just in case her daddy might need it someday."

"No." I gestured toward the couch. "We'll use that throw rug."

She seemed to like the sound of that. "We'll wrap him up like Cleopatra getting ready to surprise Julius Caesar."

Since she looked a little like Liz Taylor, back in the day, that observation seemed fitting.

"We better get dressed," I said, "and get the fuck out of here."

We did that. This process included wrapping up our unknown invader in the geometric carpet, securing him with mailing twine, and putting him in Lu's trunk.

"Second stiff today," she observed, "getting a free ride."

"You should start charging," I said.

And we left my daughter's modernistic home behind, still looking like a storm had thrashed it, and we didn't even bother cleaning up the blood and grue from the floor. I figured when we got Susan back—and *goddamnit, we would*—we'd return for a good old-fashioned house-cleaning.

I'd bring the bleach.

FIVE

Leaving the rug-wrapped would-be ninja in the trunk, we went back in and exited through the kitchen, cautiously, handguns at the ready, to check the lay of the land. The possibility of a backup man lying in wait could not be ruled out. On the other hand, the gunshots would likely have summoned him inside or sent him scurrying, so the risk was minimal. And if the dead intruder had come alone by car, there was no sign of it.

My breath smoked in the chill. "The local cops will find the abandoned car and eventually connect it to the body that'll turn up in the boonies. I don't see them linking this to us or Susan."

"No," Lu agreed, "we should be fine."

We went back to the Lexus. It was close to three A.M. now, and cold. Getting colder all the time.

With me behind the wheel, we took Highway 6 out of the Quad Cities and caught Interstate 80, taking a brief side trip into the sticks at Walcott to find the kind of lonely country road just longing for a corpse. We made its dream come true, leaving our well-stuffed rug in a ditch as promised, and I turned the driving over to Lu, doing my best to catch some more sleep. I notice I need naps, at my age, when I've exerted myself.

Other than our brief excursion into the country, the trip back to Sylvan Lake was all four-lane and an easy enough ride but for the length of it. Almost eight hours had elapsed by the time we were nearing home. We hadn't stopped except for an occasional pee break, and before cutting over to Sylvan Lake we pulled in at the 371 Diner in Baxter to grab some lunch at the old-fashioned chrome boxcar restaurant. It was after eleven A.M. now.

The place was busy for off-season, the interior a red-and-white and pink-neon-trimmed, self-consciously retro affair. Normally I got a kind of kick out of it. Right now it made my head hurt a little.

Despite the length of our journey, Lu and I hadn't talked much. We were trading off driving chores every couple of hours. Right now we were groggy from the sort of sleep you get in those circumstances. Coffee and a Diet Coke woke us up, gradually.

"Do we think," I said, as we waited in a booth for our food, "Susan was grabbed around here someplace, shortly after she left my digs? She certainly didn't make it back to Davenport."

Lu was already nodding. She looked older now, wearing no makeup, her hair less sleek, but she was still striking. "Yes. Around here somewhere. That might mean someone saw it go down."

"I do have a friend or two on the local PD I could check with."

A sculpted eyebrow rose. "When did you start slumming?"

"Hey, I'm just a solid citizen now."

"Senior citizen, you mean." She leaned forward, keeping her voice down. "Quarry, the last thing we want or Susan needs is police attention."

"Probably right. I never called 911 in my life, now that you mention it."

Our food came. I had the chopped steak with grilled onions and Lu had a BLT. Whatever else we were, we were hungry, and our conversation degenerated to the pass-the-salt-pass-the-ketchup variety.

When we'd finished, we allowed her coffee and my Diet Coke to be refreshed and we talked again.

I asked, "Do you think the late, very unlamented Duval worked with a partner?"

The setup, as least back in my day, had been passive and active. The passive half of a team would go in ahead and do recon, get the subject's patterns down and gather research, then pass that information along to the active half, who did the wet work.

Sometimes the passive member hung around and provided backup, when that was thought to be needed. Going after somebody like me, a guy who'd been in the killing business himself, might seem to call for that.

"Not everybody works in teams these days," Lu said. "Not even the ones who worked with the brokers, which is where that approach came from."

"But some still do?"

She accompanied her shrug with a nod. "Some still do. But we'd almost certainly have had the backup to deal with by now."

"Maybe that was him back at Susan's placc?"

She smirked. "What, he followed us from here to the Quad Cities before taking us on?"

"Well, what was he doing there, then?"

This shrug was more elaborate. "Probably he was who searched the place earlier. Back for a second pass. We can't exactly ask him."

"No. No we can't."

She sipped her coffee. She took it black. Lu did not kid around. "You spent several days with her, Quarry. Didn't your baby girl tell you anything about what she was working on?"

I shook my head. "Just what I told you before. Which was very close to jack shit."

Lu stared at me over the rim of her coffee cup. "Think back. What did Susan say that could be useful? Because I can't think of much to try, other than to backtrack through a couple of brokers your caller might have been working with."

"That would be a path."

She gave me an unblinking look. "A tedious one, and I'd be exposed as, you know, not all that dead."

"Can't ask you to risk that. But you could guide me where to go."

"I could. Let's consider that option, at least. But are there any other cards to play? Think! What did Susan say when she left, besides 'goodbye' and maybe let you know what a great father you've been lately? The first forty years, not so much."

That made me smile. Probably should have made me mad, but it was just so Lu.

"The last thing she said," I said, "was...shit!"

She frowned. "The last thing she said was 'shit'?"

"No, no. The last thing Susan said was she needed gas before she headed out. She asked me if maybe I could fix her up at the lodge's convenience store pumps. But we don't keep the tanks full during the off-season."

Lu was nodding, slowly. "So she stopped somewhere, in the area, before taking off home."

"Right."

"A good opportunity for somebody to grab her."

"Right."

Another frown. "How many gas stations are there around here? I mean, it's a goddamn tourist area."

"Well, she'd be heading over to Highway 371. That would take her from Sylvan to Baxter, which is right where we are. To get to the highway, there's a Holiday station she'd pass right by."

"That would be a good place to start."

So we did.

The Holiday station had four pumps under its canopy and despite its name wasn't all that festive. It had the look of a place waiting for just the right moment to go out of business. But it sat on a big chunk of blacktop that served as a parking lot, which right now had one vehicle in it...

...a Cadillac CT 5. Silver.

Maybe it wasn't Susan's car. There were other Cadillac CT 5's in the world, after all, even silver ones. This might not have been hers...if the Iowa license plate hadn't sealed it.

I asked Lu, "Do you know how to pick a car door lock?"

She grunted a laugh. "Not without a set of lockpicks I don't."

"With lockpicks you do?"

"What do you think?"

I gave her my packet of picks, which I'd grabbed before leaving for Susan's last night. I was a Boy Scout, you know.

I was already heading into the gas station. "See if there's anything in there. I'm going to talk to the clerk."

She went to work on the door lock with the picks. I liked that she knew just which ones to go to.

They say it's better to be lucky than smart, and all I can say is this time I was lucky. The kid in the light-blue Holiday blouse behind the counter was the only employee on duty, apparently. He was concentrating on trying to grow a beard and not doing that well, his pimples peeking out like berries on a bush. But he happened to have been working the evening Susan disappeared.

I showed him a five-dollar bill. "You see anything unusual yesterday afternoon?"

He pretended to ignore the five, as if it were beneath him. "No. It was steady. Plenty of people goin' home after Christmas."

"Anybody report anything?"

"Like what?"

"Like a scuffle in the parking lot. Maybe like a woman getting stuffed into a car against her will."

"That would be like a kidnapping."

"That would be exactly like a kidnapping."

He frowned; his eyebrows were dark and bushy and met in the middle as if working out a truce. "You wouldn't be a cop?"

"Yes, I wouldn't be a cop. But I am a guy with a five-dollar bill."

"Well, that's not much of a bribe, mister."

"I'm not bribing you. This is not a bribe. Google it. This is a fair exchange. Information for money. I'm asking if you saw something, or if somebody reported something that went down in the parking lot."

"Nobody did. That I know of, anyway. Is that enough information?"

"No. Do you have a security camera?"

"Yes. We got half a dozen. They're all around, mostly outside."

I smiled, suddenly a pal. "I might have a twenty for you, if you let me look at the tape."

"I said we got cameras. I didn't say they was, like, turned on."

I studied him trying to grow his beard. "Why wouldn't you turn them on?"

"The manager says just the cameras are detergent enough."

"You mean deterrent."

"Do I?"

I gave him the five.

Outside, Lu had the car doors open, including the trunk, which yawned in its emptiness.

"Nothing," she said. "Not a damn thing. What now?"

"We'll take the Caddy with us. You drive."

"Do you know how to hot-wire a car?"

"What do you think?"

We were a little grouchy, after all we'd been through.

Back in my glorified cabin, I built a fire and we sat in front of it in the chairs that yesterday's caller and I had occupied not long ago.

"So they grabbed her on this end," Lu said.

"Yes. At the Holiday station. She came to spend the holiday with me and got taken at the Holiday station. Is that ironic or just stupid?"

"I wouldn't know." Lu was thinking. "Does that mean she's being *kept* around here?"

"Not necessarily. Maybe that's the case—if I get a ransom call."

"You don't *really* think this is about ransom, do you?"

"No. Hell no. My answer machine isn't blinking red, so it doesn't think so either."

"What now?"

I glanced at her and the grouchiness, on my part anyway, receded. "This isn't about you, Lu. I appreciate what you've done. Very much. You've made what's been accomplished possible."

"Which isn't very fucking much."

I gestured with an open hand. "We determined somebody was looking for something at Susan's place. We found her car. And don't forget, we thinned the competition—Duval and the ski-mask ninja are off the game board."

"Don't forget I helped you with the driving." Was that sarcasm in her voice? "And we used my car."

"No. Thank you for that, too."

Lu sprang to her feet and came over and shook a finger at

me like the world's most unlikely schoolteacher. "You left out I saved your ass! You left out I killed a guy and I'm your accomplice killing another asshole last night. You left out that I'm in this up to my twat and you have no right to send me packing."

I curled my finger at her. She moved closer. I pointed to my lap and said, "Sit."

She did.

Lu was a lot of woman to do that, legs everywhere and she had to put her arms around my neck to maintain balance. But she did it.

"I appreciate what you've done," I told her. "I just want you to know I don't expect any more of you. If you want to play Sancho Panza in a push-up bra, that's fine with me. I appreciate it. But we haven't seen each other in, what? Twenty years? I don't expect you to lay your lovely ass on the line for me any more than you already have."

Her face had stayed blank throughout my little speech, but now she began to smile. No teeth, just a curling thing at either end.

"You're sweet," she said.

She kissed me.

I kissed her back.

"But I don't wear a bra," Lu said, grinding my groin with her bottom, "push-up or otherwise. Why, do you think I need one? If my tits need pushing up, don't you think I can find somebody to do it for me?"

Somehow she managed to arrange herself with her head on my shoulder and we stayed that way a while. She fell asleep— I could tell from the gentle snoring—but I didn't. My mind wouldn't let go. And I couldn't seem to get comfortable.

She stirred against me.

"I thought of something," I said, and moved to get up. She

pried herself loose from me and watched as I went to the phone on the kitchen counter. I dialed digits off a sheet of frequently called numbers.

Lu came over and listened, leaning an elbow against the counter.

"Charles," I said to my editor, "do you happen to know who Susan Breedlove's literary agent is?...Good....Good." I wrote the number down. "Thank you! Thank you."

I turned toward Lu. "If I get this guy, I'll put it on speaker. But just listen, okay?"

She made a "zip" motion with two fingers across the lips.

"Manhattan Literary Agency," a female voice said.

"Is Mr. Davis in?"

"Who may I say is calling, sir?"

"I'm the father of one of his clients—Susan Breedlove."

That got her attention.

"Let me see if he's available."

It wasn't long before a husky male voice said, "So you're Susan's father! You must be very proud."

"I am. But I'm concerned because she's dropped off the grid."

"Well, that shouldn't be surprising. Journalists, and that's what true-crime authors are, often drop out of sight, pursuing a lead."

"That's what concerns me. After all, as I'm sure you know, her subject matter is dangerous."

"Yes, of course, it is...but I wouldn't worry, Mister, uh... Breedlove is it?"

"Yes. Breedlove."

The voice was confident and almost patronizing. "Susan can take care of herself, and she's also well-known enough at this point that no one's going to give her any trouble."

Tell that to John Lennon.

"I hope you're right," I said. "Would you happen to know what project she's working on now?"

"Well, what I *can* tell you is that she has a book contract, the final book on a three-book deal."

"A book contract on what subject?"

He chuckled. "True crime, of course."

"*What* true crime, Mr. Davis?"

"An author as successful as your daughter, Mr. Breedlove, is allowed to play her cards close to the vest. Even the publisher doesn't know what the new book is about, and not her editor, not even her agent...*me*...knows anything more than that it will lay open another horrific crime that will set America on its collective ear."

I thanked him and hung up by way of the speaker phone button. I gave the phone the finger, then looked glumly at Lu.

"Shit," I said. "Dead end."

Both those sculpted eyebrows were up. "It does further back up that this is probably something to do with the crime or crimes she's been researching of late."

I nodded. "But there's no sign anyone's broken in here, and this is where Susan had been staying over Christmas."

Lu gestured around us. "That probably was what your caller, Duval, was supposed to do once he'd taken you out—shake this place down. But looking for what?"

"Well, she had her laptop with her. So when she was grabbed, they would've got that as well."

"If they have her laptop," Lu said, "isn't that all they need? Right there would be her book in progress, her research, her e-mails. So why did they toss her house last night?"

I grunted. "They probably want any kind of backup she might have left, a flash drive possibly, or a password and instructions on how to get her backed-up materials off the cloud."

The almond eyes narrowed. "Do you expect whoever is

behind this to send someone here to confront you? And to
search this place for anything Susan may have left here, or
hidden on the premises?"

"Possibly. Whoever hired Duval knows he didn't return from
his mission, successful and alive. Nor did the man they sent to
search Susan's house. And some of them know who I am, and
the threat I present…even at this ripe old age."

Lu threw a hand in the air. "So, what? Just stay put and let
them come to us?" But then frowned in thought. "…Maybe
that's not such a bad idea. They don't know about me. They
don't know it's *two* old pros they're dealing with."

I grinned at her and it had an edge. "Let's go with that. I
have plenty of armament, and I can show you where I've
stowed guns all around this place. We can go *Straw Dogs* on
their asses if need be, and all we need is one of them alive to
lead us to Susan."

"If they don't come tonight," Lu said, eyebrows up again,
"they may not come at all."

Now I threw a hand in the air. "So we give it one night, and
then we go calling on a broker or two, and backtrack Duval."

"Agreed."

I fixed us a couple of medium-rare steaks and made some
American fries and we drank wine. It was about as romantic an
evening as you can have, waiting for somebody to come try to
kill you. We hadn't talked at all about the reality of what Susan
might be going through: if she had something they wanted,
information, a manuscript, a combination thereof, she faced
torture and/or psychoactive drugs working as truth serum. And
once Susan talked, she'd be of no use and would be just another
chapter in somebody else's true-crime book.

It had been a rough, long twenty-four hours or so. I took a
bath, after which she showered. I fell into bed around eight,

tucking my nine mil under my pillow again. I could hear her showering across the way. Then she was framed in the doorway, tall, tanned, her black hair damp tendrils, her busty slender frame wrapped up in a terrycloth robe.

"I'll do all the work," she said.

"Okay," I said.

The robe dropped away, puddling to her feet; she stepped out of it, showing off a vintage female frame that any twenty-year-old babe would have killed for.

She flipped the covers off me and knelt between my legs and her head went down and bobbed up and went down and bobbed up. Soon she was on top of me. I filled my face with those breasts and my hands with the globes of her ass and slipped up inside of her, the rhythmic, hypnotic movement building to a satisfying finish, which she topped off with a kiss on the lips.

Then she hopped off of me and the bed, went toward the door, plucking up the robe as she went. She was in the bathroom a while and returned in the robe again and curled up beside me like a big, purring cat.

I fell asleep, but something in the back of my brain refused to become a dream and instead formed a thought that woke me as if an alarm clock had gone off.

Maybe Susan had left something in the guest room.

I scrambled there in my bare feet.

And there it was on her nightstand: a small envelope that said "Jack" on it, in her handwriting. I opened it quickly. It said:

> *"Dad,*
>
> > *If something happens,*
> > *you are my backup.*
> >
> > > *Susan"*

No flash drive, no computer passwords, nothing new from her to give me a path now. I would check the drive with the *Sniper 2* manuscript later and come up empty. No, she was invoking "backup" in the hit team sense. But I was struck, nonetheless, by her addressing me as "Dad." Half of my mouth almost smiled.

Then Lu was in the doorway, saying, "There you are!"

"Yeah. Nothing here, really."

She came over to me quickly. "I got up to go to the bathroom."

"I do that sometimes."

Her eyes were impossibly wide; she clutched my arm. "I saw something. Out the window."

"What?"

"Do you keep any lights on in the resort hotel?"

"Not this time of year."

"Well, there's one on right now in a second-floor window."

SIX

The view from my bedroom window at the rear of my two-story cabin faced the lodge building half a block away, separated from it by a grassy plot of land I kept trimmed during warm weather and a big blacktop parking lot beyond. The former was somewhat overgrown now and wore a light snowfall like a thread-bare garment; the latter extended to the rear of the lodge, much bigger than the hotel's dozen rooms required, designed to service our popular restaurant, which in-season attracted plenty of tourists, far more than our limited lodgings could accommodate.

The full moon gave the outdoors an ivory cast. Right now, the parking lot was deserted but for a layer of snow—José hadn't plowed it yet—with not even a single solitary vehicle to represent our unexpected guest, announced by the soft yellow glow coming through sheer curtains on a second-floor window in the otherwise slumbering building.

"That's either Duval's backup making an overdue appearance," I said, lowering binoculars, "or his broker sent somebody to check up on the situation."

I'd detected no movement behind that jaundiced glow.

"Well," Lu said next to me, still in the terrycloth robe, a hand on my shoulder, "either way, it's obviously a trap."

Whether her gesture spoke of affection or apprehension, I couldn't tell you.

I frowned. "Yes, but what trap exactly? Am I expected to check out that light in the window and get jumped? Or get shot on my way there, courtesy of a lurker in the trees? Or maybe some bastard is just waiting with a gun, either in that room or some other one on the second floor, ready to tap my ass?"

"Six of one," she said with a shrug.

I faced her. Her hand fell away from my shoulder, but I put my left hand on her right shoulder. "Ambushing me is a definite possibility. But if I were whoever this is, I'd figure the situation could be controlled better inside. Either way, we can't ignore this invitation."

"Agreed," Lu said. The almond eyes were calm. "What's the layout?"

I gave her a quick rundown of the unpretentious, rustic accommodations upstairs at the lodge—a single floor of rooms with bath for well-off guests who liked to think they were roughing it. We defined roughing it at the Sylvan Lodge by way of no TV and furnishings that were the latest thing circa 1967. We did provide (costly) room service.

I intended to provide my own variety of that myself, including the costly part.

"Get dressed," I told her, "but leave the lights off."

She nodded and set about doing that. Her getaway bag was here in my bedroom and she got into navy blue slacks and sweater and low-heel boots while I climbed into a black sweatshirt and blue jeans and running shoes, not that I did much running these days.

On the two shelves of my closet were a dozen carrying cases for pistols, coated gray steel lined with foam padding with fitted cut-outs for specific weapons. About half were empty, representing the handguns salted around the place. The rest represented an assortment with specific needs in mind, from long barrels to sniper scopes.

I selected a Glock 22, like the law enforcement personnel around here carried. The weapon took the same ammo as my nine mil, which would make my life easier. I got into a shoulder holster and filled it with the nine mil from under my pillow. Then I looped a belt through my jeans and added a hip holster for the Glock, tucking that in place.

"Well aren't we loaded for bear," Lu said, dryly amused.

"Actually," I said, "I'm probably the 'bear' in this scenario. You can take a pass on this one, you know."

"It's not nice, you insulting me."

"Sorry."

"I didn't take you for a gun nut."

"I'm not a gun nut. I don't particularly like guns. I'm a gun nut like a carpenter is a hammer and screwdriver enthusiast."

She nodded. "Tools of the trade."

I shrugged. "Tools of the trade."

From my nightstand drawer, I grabbed three nine-millimeter clips (that's "magazines," for you anal-retentive types) and stuffed them in a front jeans pocket.

I said to her, "You're not going to like what I do next."

"I'll try not to lose my shit," she said.

My cell was on the nightstand and I punched in the number of the Sylvan PD, which may surprise you to learn I'd committed to memory. The six-officer outfit operated out of City Hall; I knew everyone on the small department. I was the manager of a popular local resort, after all.

I asked the dispatcher, whose name was Ellen, who was on patrol tonight. She was a cute redhead with a Betty Boop voice, and once when I'd pointed out the vocal resemblance, she said she'd never heard of Betty What's-It. Kids today, no sense of history.

On patrol tonight was Ben Loomis, a Black guy in his early twenties who had graduated from Minnesota State a few years ago with a Law Enforcement degree. Kind of a know-it-all and pain-in-ass, though, and if he'd taken a better personality into his job interviews, he'd have landed a position at a bigger department.

"I may have an intruder at the lodge," I told Ellen. "Send Ben around, would you?"

"Roger that."

Wasn't that cute?

I said, "Ask Officer Loomis to meet me at the lodge convenience store."

That confused her. "I thought you weren't open this time of year."

"That's right. Lights'll be off. Speaking of which, tell Loomis no siren or flashers. I'm more interested in catching the prowler than scaring him away."

"Roger that."

Gotta love it.

I clicked off and Lu asked, "What are you up to?"

"Stirring the pot," I said.

She followed me into the living room, where I got my fur-collared jacket out of the front closet. She slipped into the black topcoat she'd inherited from the late Duval, watching me curiously.

What was I up to?

The far side of the lane that took you to my glorified cabin was lined with towering pines, their green clumped with white like faux-Christmas-tree flocking. A network of narrow lanes wove through the mini-forest, home to half a dozen guest cabins, all vacant at the moment, unless my intruder—and possibly an accomplice—was only pretending to inhabit the lodge and had been keeping an eye on me from these woods.

Wouldn't be the first time.

That meant taking care as we edged along the line of trees,

past the plot of land behind my dwelling and then through the vast empty parking lot beyond that. We took our time, walking just inside the tree line. I took the lead and had Lu keep checking behind us, with her walking backward half of the time, so we had to move slow.

But no trap was sprung in the trees, meaning our host must be waiting inside, likely on the second floor, as I'd speculated. Still, I doubted he'd be in that end-of-the-hall room whose light-in-the-window had summoned us. More likely he'd pop out of one of the other rooms at right or left.

When we were parallel to the lodge building itself, I led Lu quickly across the lane to the back of the building, the moon a prison searchlight threatening our capture. But we made it without incident to the restaurant entrance off the parking lot. Centered on the rear wall, the double door had a standard knob lock, a stainless-steel number I'd installed myself earlier this year. It bore fresh scratches that indicated I wasn't the only guy around with a packet of lockpicks.

Lu and I exchanged looks, hers a frown. She seemed to be wondering if I could seriously be considering going in this way myself, as our intruder clearly had. Which of course would have made sitting ducks out of us.

I shook my head and pointed toward the street side of the building.

We headed around to the front, staying close to the outer brick wall, with me still leading the way. I paused at the building's edge, peeked around and saw our six pumps—two more than the Holiday station—under their canopy, bathed by a pair of high-up security lights. The canopied pumps were down at right, where the convenience store took up the front far-end corner of the structure.

Staying close to the building, we headed down there. My key

ring was in my left-side jacket pocket and I fished it out with my free hand, my right occupied by the Glock 22. I'm ambidextrous enough to work a key in a lock with my left, which I quietly did, then held the door open for Lu and followed her inside.

During the winter we kept the heat on in the lodge, but just enough to avoid pipes from freezing, so it was damn cold in there. The only lighting within came from some coolers and a fountain pop machine, serving as security lighting. The counter with register was at the right as you came in, the shelving and displays lined up before you like soldiers at parade rest. Any perishable food had been removed and only the packaged items remained. Most of that crap wouldn't spoil till nothing was left on the planet but cockroaches and the Rolling Stones.

An SUV rolled in, a dark blue Ford Expedition, beneath whose side windows were white letters that said

SYLVAN

over bigger white-edged light-blue letters that said

POLICE

announcing Officer Ben Loomis, who got out and came around with a swagger that went well with his Richard Roundtree mustache. He was bare-headed, his hair cropped close.

In his navy-blue bomber jacket, unzipped revealing his light blue shirt, its twin breast pockets edged in dark blue, his slacks dark blue as well, Loomis worked hard at exuding a gunslinger's confidence. His right hand rode the butt of his hip-holstered Glock 22. I knew for a fact he'd never been in a shooting situation. He had not served in the military and the ghetto he grew up in was an upper-middle-class housing division in Brainerd.

I pushed open the door and waved him into the sleeping store. In he strode.

"Sitrep, Jack," he said. He was keeping his voice down.

Lu gave me a glance.

"The situation," I reported softly, and nodded toward Lu, "is my friend here noticed a light on in an upstairs window on the hotel-room floor."

"That would be the rear of the building."

"Yes."

"And this is off-season."

"Correct." I gestured to Lu. "This is Louise Petersen." That was the name she was using on this trip.

"Miz Petersen," Officer Loomis said with a nod and no eye contact. "Jack, I need you and your lady friend to stay here while I deal with this."

"Sure," I said.

His voice got stern. "I realize you like to handle problems yourself, and that you're king of the roost around here...but this is police business."

"Understood."

"This isn't like that thing last fall. That wasn't any way to handle a situation like that."

I had shot a racoon that was getting into our garbage.

"I'm sorry about that," I said. I'd apologized for that particular homicide a number of times already.

He raised a pointing finger. "This isn't anything a civilian should be handling."

"You mean this break-in. Or are we still talking about the racoon?"

I delivered that completely deadpan and it flew right over the officer's head. Lu twitched a smile, though. He didn't seem to notice.

"The break-in, of course," he snapped. "Did you get a look at him?"

"Just a glimpse." Which of course I hadn't. "But I think he had a gun."

"A gun. What kind of gun?"

"Just some kind of handgun. I don't know anything about that kind of thing."

Did I mention my fur-collared black leather jacket came down over the Glock 22 on my hip and of course concealed my shoulder-holstered Browning nine mil as well?

"I'm just saying," I said, "you need to CYA."

Using him as a stalking horse was one thing, sending him in unawares was another.

Officer Loomis got his Glock 22 out and, to his credit, held it with the barrel pointed straight up, though in a two-handed grip that overdid it. He was not a bad officer—just full of himself and officious. Neither being qualities that endeared him to me, I admit.

But in this situation he was exactly who I wanted to have walking point. I'd encouraged the gun because I knew something he didn't: what kind of "prowler" was up there.

"Now, remember," Loomis said, "you people stay here. I will handle this."

He started off and I put a hand on his arm and stopped him. Gently, but I stopped him, and he flashed me an irritated look.

"Yes?" he said.

"Where are you headed?"

"Up the stairs, of course."

The restaurant's payment station and the hotel's check-in/check-out desk shared a long counter, just inside the parking lot entrance. This was beyond the back wall of coolers and not directly accessible from here. Loomis would have to go down a brief corridor of restrooms on the other side of the convenience store. The corridor emptied into the restaurant's entry area with the wide staircase that had apparently been designed to provide our roughing-it guests with plenty of room to carry their own luggage up.

"You might," I suggested to the officer, "use the rear stairs that come out in the supply closet. The fire stairs off the kitchen? You'd have an element of surprise that going up the front way wouldn't provide."

"Jack," Loomis said, with a toothy, patronizing grin, "your tactical advice is appreciated, but I think I know what I'm doing. Just the sight of a uniformed officer will shut something like this down in a heartbeat."

A last heartbeat, maybe.

"Go for it," I said supportively.

He headed over to the little corridor of facing restrooms. I almost suggested he stop and make a deposit, considering what might follow, but thought better of it.

As we stood there in the hibernating convenience store, Lu gave me a look.

"He's an idiot," she said, "isn't he?"

"Oh yeah."

"You knew that when you heard he was the officer on patrol, didn't you?"

"Don't tell anybody."

Loomis, going up that way, would enter into a wide hallway with rooms facing each other at left and right, and one at the far end overlooking the parking lot: the guest room where a light was on. Any presumption that this was where our intruder remained seemed ill-advised—he could easily be in any other of those rooms on either side of the corridor, lying in wait for yours truly. Or whatever advance agent yours truly might have dispatched....

I almost felt a little guilty. This time it would be a professional killer, not a racoon.

"What now?" Lu asked. "Wait around for him to fuck things up? Maybe help ourselves to some fine Hostess products?"

A muffled gunshot from above us seemed to answer her.

"Come with me," I said, already on the move.

We quickly went from the convenience store into the check-in area, the same way Loomis had gone, only we skirted the wide wooden stairway with its elaborate banisters that he'd taken.

Damn near running, I led Lu into and through the spacious dining room on the parking lot side. Some limited security lighting revealed chairs upended, their bottoms resting on tabletops, legs in the air like chorus girls frozen mid-kick.

As manager of the lodge, just checking up on things, I was obviously in here from time to time during off-season—both the convenience store and the restaurant. But seldom this time of year had I been inside either one at night, and the chilly temperature and limited lighting made the entire facility feel different, which gave off an overall haunted-house vibe. It was as if we'd gone out of business while nobody was looking, or perhaps this was the zombie apocalypse and nothing much was left but the imminent arrival of the marauding dead.

The kitchen was to the right and between it and the dining room was the fire exit stairwell—the back way up. Lu was so close behind me as we ascended the darkened stairs, I could hear her breathe, hell, I could *feel* her breathe. We emerged in a medium-size closet with shelves of supplies on one side and bedding on the other; this put us between two guest rooms. I cracked the door, the Glock 22's nose up—I was not gripping the weapon in two hands, though.

Where the front stairway emptied out, Loomis was crumpled on the floor, a pile of blue leaking red; he was twitching and groaning. He appeared to have got it in the belly.

And a figure in black and a black ski mask—what, were they issuing this shit from some secret hitman headquarters?—was ducking in a door on the left side of the hall, the room next to the one at the end where the light burned yellow. He did not seem to have seen me cracking the supply-closet door for a look before he sealed himself in.

I slipped out of the closet; Lu was right behind me, her gun-in-hand barrel up, too.

I whispered, barely audible, "Wait till I signal you. Then tear down this corridor, toward the lit room. Really slap shoe leather."

To her credit, she had not a single question for me about what might have seemed a stupid and dangerous task for her. She trusted me. I damn near loved her for it. And I will freely admit I was fond of this woman. I always had been, even on that first job when I'd been sent to kill her and couldn't quite bring myself to do it.

I used my big toes to pry myself out of my running shoes. Then, very quietly—on little fucking cat feet—I moved down the hall on the opposite side from where Loomis lay bleeding and twitching. I arrived at the last door on the left—which had an appropriate horror movie ring, don't you think?—and positioned myself against the wall.

I looked over at Lu, who had the supply closet door halfway open now, waiting for her cue.

With a nod, I gave it to her.

And she ran, pounding the floor with her feet as she went, ridiculously loud, and that was all it took—the door next to me began to open and, standing safely angled, I fired three times into it. The gun, not wearing a noise suppressor, made explosive reports punctuated by the cracking of the wood they blasted through.

I backed away and the door opened wider and he stumbled out. He fell to his knees. And he fell on his face.

He wasn't dead. He was breathing hard but not his last, though like Loomis he was soaking in his own spreading blood, which between the two scarlet messes they were making would mean I'd have to replace this indoor/outdoor carpeting before the season started. Well, better it than me.

I checked him for weapons and the only one he had was a .22, a Winchester Auto, which I immediately collected.

Across the way, Lu was kneeling over the fallen Loomis, who wasn't twitching any more.

"Mine's alive," I said. "How's the officer?"

"He's alive. Gone sleepy-bye, but alive. Is that a good thing or a bad thing?"

"A good thing." I didn't want him dead. Using him as bait was quite enough.

She came over to me, nodded toward this latest assassin in black. "Who's this?"

I had pulled off the ski mask. He was on his belly so I had to bend down and turn his head toward her. Our unregistered guest was bald with a trimmed beard, pale as death, but he was living all right. Breathing like a champ.

"Never saw him before," I said. Not that there was anything remarkable about him. "How about you?"

Crouching over him, she shrugged. "After my time, I guess. Anyway, nobody who ever worked for me. You wanted him alive to question, so that's good."

"Yeah. How bad is the officer?"

"Midsection, but not necessarily fatal. He could be lucky—getting gut-shot is usually a one-way ticket." She grunted a laugh. "I'm not sure someone this dumb should be allowed to live."

"Don't be like that."

Her look was amused. "When did you grow a conscience, Quarry?"

"Oh, hell, I've always been a softie." I got to my feet and dug my cell phone out of my jeans. "Now if you want to see a first, stay tuned—I'm about to call 911 and get Officer Loomis some medical care."

She rose with a smile. "You *are* a changed man."

SEVEN

The next morning, nearing ten A.M., Lu and I sat on the couch where on Christmas Eve I'd exchanged gifts with Susan in front of the fake pine and its twinkling white lights. The tree was still up but the lights weren't plugged in, and the couch had been moved into its usual position with its back to Ol' Tannenbaum. Pulled around to face us in the comfy chair where not long ago the now-dead Duval had sat was a plain-clothes investigator from the Brainerd PD.

They were handling the incident because the Sylvan police didn't have an investigator on staff. And the Brainerd Department was a much bigger operation, after all—they had a whop-ping four investigators. This was the senior officer on the investigative team, Carl Goedkin, in his mid-fifties with short gray hair and a gray-and-black mustache and a bland expres-sion. His off-the-rack suit looked rumpled and so did he, having been up through the wee hours dealing with the crime. We'd been temporarily dismissed last night, and this was our first in-depth interview.

"So what is it you do in Billings, Miss Petersen?" he asked in a weary baritone.

"Not much except occasionally travel," Lu said. "Now and then a theater trip." She'd already told him she was a retired schoolteacher from Boulder.

And she looked like one, in a modest white blouse and navy slacks, her dark hair back in a short ponytail, her face free of makeup, almond eyes minimized by tortoiseshell horn-rim reading glasses.

"I moved to Billings," she volunteered, "because the, uh, friend I lived with for many years, another schoolteacher, passed away and it was just too difficult for me to...well, I needed fresh surroundings."

This was all part of the new life she'd bought herself after she "died."

"I understand," he replied in a way that said he didn't.

"Jack and I are old friends," she said. "He's a shirttail relation of Lily's. Grew up with her in Boulder."

"Lily?"

"My late schoolteacher, uh...friend."

"Ah," the detective said, finally putting the clues together.

We'd already told him that neither of us had witnessed the shooting, that we'd been downstairs in the convenience store where Officer Loomis had told us to wait, instructions we'd obeyed till we heard the shot.

"I'm a little puzzled, Miss Petersen," Goedkin said, "that you went up to the second floor with Mr. Keller. You'd have been safer downstairs."

"Oh, Jack was armed, remember, and I felt safer staying with him."

The detective knew I'd brought along my licensed nine millimeter to look into a break-in. He'd taken a few moments at the scene to check for signs that the gun might have been fired, sniffing the barrel and opening the chamber to sniff that, too. And of course it hadn't been fired since my last shooting range visit, over a month ago.

I'd of course played a little game of mix-and-match with the extra Glock 22 I'd brought along the night before. I'd exchanged my discharged one for the unconscious Loomis's identical but unfired weapon, which right now was living in a gun case in my closet. The one with which I'd blasted away at that hotel-room door I'd left in the out-cold cop's limp grasp. The only risk was somebody checking serial numbers—neither Glock had any other identifying mark.

Oh, and after I put the gun in Loomis's hand, and grasped his loose grip, I put my forefinger over his in the trigger guard and fired off one round at the wall near the bullet-blistered door, just to leave some gunshot residue confirming he'd shot the thing.

"Officer Loomis is conscious," Goedkin said, "but he's still pretty dazed. He doesn't even remember firing his weapon."

"My guess," I said, "is the perp got the first shot off and—as Loomis was going down—your brave officer reflexively returned fire before hitting the floor."

"Of course," Lu said, with just a trace of a smile and a whole lot of helpful attitude, "we didn't *see* that. We didn't get up there till the shooting was over."

Goedkin seemed to be having no trouble accepting any of this. He'd been recording us on his cell phone, which he now retrieved and shut off and tucked away. He gave us a somber look. "You folks owe Officer Loomis a big debt of thanks."

"We sure do," I said.

Lu pretended to be confused. "Why is that, Detective Goedkin?"

He flipped a hand, which after his long night seemed to take some effort. "Well, we've already had a kickback from the NCIC database. Your invader was a dangerous individual—two arrests and one conviction on armed-robbery charges. Clarence Whitlock, that's his name, was part of a robbery team that hit a bank in Elgin, Illinois, in 2010. Did four years in Joliet. Who knows what might have happened last night if Officer Loomis hadn't been on the job."

I asked, just curious of course, "What sort of shape is this Whitlock in?"

Goedkin let out a sigh that seemed to start at his toes. "Officer Loomis fired off four rounds, apparently, two hitting the suspect, who took one bullet in the chest between the left shoulder and heart, and another in the right shoulder." Goedkin smiled a little. "I hope his hobby isn't tennis....But even so, he was lucky. They were clean shots, in and out."

Which was total happenstance. I was surprised I hadn't killed the prick. But I wasn't sorry I hadn't. That meant, if I could get next to him, I might pry some information out of Mr. Whitlock that could lead us to Susan.

Lu had her hands folded and draped between her legs as she leaned forward. "What about Officer Loomis?"

"He was *really* lucky. Missed his intestines, which could have been a horrible way to die. Another in-and-out, straight through-and-through shot."

I asked innocently, "Where is the officer? I'd like to visit him, when it's time, and thank him for what he did."

"He's at St. Joseph's in Brainerd. So, for that matter, is the notorious Clarence Whitlock. But with a police guard on his door."

I frowned, just a good solid citizen who had never encountered such things before. "You expecting somebody who isn't a friendly guest?"

Goedkin got to his feet and so did we.

"According to the NCIC readout," he said, "Whitlock has some very nasty known associates. Shooting an officer adds to the severity of the felony charges he'll face, and that makes any accomplices he might've had, a getaway driver for example, guilty of everything he is. One of his cronies might like to see him leave the hospital in a body bag, before he could implicate anybody." He nodded at Lu, giving her a mildly embarrassed smile. "Excuse the rough talk, ma'am."

"That's all right, Detective," she said. "No rougher than my Middle School students used to be."

That made him chuckle. At the door, he gave us both nods and said there might be follow-up; be sure to let him know if we—or either of us—were leaving town. We said we would.

Back on the couch, Lu tossed the glasses on an end table, sat on her legs and undid her ponytail, shook her scythes of dark hair back in place. "That's quite an interrogation technique."

I leaned back. "You mean where we give the cop next to nothing and the cop empties the bag?"

"Correct." She folded her arms and the almond eyes disappeared into slits. "Tell me something."

"Okay."

Her head cocked. "You could hardly have anticipated what went down on the second floor with Officer Loomis and, what's his name, Whitlock?"

"Of course not."

Now the eyes got wide. "Yet you took along a Glock 22, like Loomis carried."

"All the cops around here pack those."

She smirked at me. "So you brought one to swap out with Loomis? Give me a break."

I shrugged. "I just thought it might come in handy. You never know when you'll have to improvise. Anyway, I figured whatever cop came around, he'd go after our caller first. And what we knew and Loomis didn't was that our caller was a…"

"Don't say 'hitman,'" she said, raising a "stop" palm. "I hate that."

"…pro. It was just a piece of luck that a dim, cocky character like Loomis caught the call."

Her grin was crooked as she shook her head and the blades of black hair traveled. "No wonder you're still alive after all these years."

"It's a gift."

She yawned, stretching, fists raised high; under the white blouse, the large breasts challenged its buttons. "Buy me breakfast?"

"Sure."

The Baxter diner's chrome exterior was trimmed in red and blue neon with three American flags flapping out front, in case you forgot what country you were in. We took a booth, and I had biscuits and gravy while Lu dug into a short stack. We had worked up an appetite last night that had followed us here.

"It would be nice," she said, daubing some syrup off her lower lip with a paper napkin, "to know who Whitlock works through."

"His broker, you mean."

"His broker. Based on his NCIC package, Whitlock appears to be a Midwestern boy, with obvious Illinois ties, and I know who the middleman is there, assuming he hasn't retired himself. He's in Naperville."

"Not a surprise. That's one of the wealthier Chicago suburbs."

"It is." She had a bite of pancake. "Name is Wallace Conlon. He'll be surprised to see me alive, which may be enough to shake him into talking. And you have a reputation in the business, kind of rare in this shadowy line of work. That 'list' business where you went around killing your own kind is what did it. Some people think you're a wild man."

"Yeah. From Borneo. And if this Conlon won't talk?"

"I think he will, with the right encouragement."

I didn't love the sound of that—I'm not much for torture. Saw too much of it in Vietnam, and anyway people will say anything to get you to stop.

She was saying, "But it could be a couple of other people,

and the next best bet is probably the Minneapolis middleman. And that's a problem for me."

"You worked around there. You're *really* supposed to be dead in the Twin Cities." I shrugged. "If it comes to that, just point me in the right direction and fade."

"Now you be quiet about that. I'm *in* this. We've been at this only a couple of days and already've dumped two stiffs and now we've got a wounded…"

"Don't say hitman. You hate that."

"…assassin in the hospital and a shot-up cop, too. My point is, I am in this up to my…"

"Tits, I think you said."

"…neck. All I'm saying is we'll have to be a little more discreet than we've been so far, if we head to my old stomping grounds."

"I think it's 'stamping,' not stomping."

That made her smile; her chin even crinkled. "You are so bad."

"I get that a lot."

We pushed our cleaned plates aside, a busboy collected them, and Lu said, "What's next?"

"Visiting hours."

St. Joseph's Medical Center in Brainerd, on North 53rd, was a multi-angle rust-brick sprawl that might have been assembled by a giant child with colossal building blocks. The two-story lobby—brown wall here, tan wall there, with olive furnishings and carpet, a bulging balcony looming over the front desk—was similarly self-consciously modern, as if being sick weren't enough, you had to be intimidated, too.

We asked at the front desk and were told Ben Loomis was on the third floor. That was not the ICU, which meant Loomis was doing well and also that we wouldn't have any bells and whistles to deal with, getting in to see him.

Moving down a pale green-walled corridor, we made our way past a busy nurse's station to Officer Loomis's room halfway down. The tile beneath our feet was a mottled green as if we were walking across a frozen swamp—good thing I was in my bomber jacket and Lu in her inherited topcoat. The distinctive bouquet of disinfectant and cleaning products, with just a hint of cafeteria, took me back to my post-double-bypass stay—a different hospital, of course, but they all smell the same.

We knocked at the patient's door and, his voice lacking the commanding, even arrogant attitude of the night before, he said, "Yes? Come?"

We went in.

He looked pretty good considering, with only a single IV feeding him antibiotics, fluids, and other medications; no patient monitor, either, as this wasn't an ICU floor, or breathing tube. The bed was not cranked up, due to the position of his wound, I supposed. The lower half of him was under a sheet and blanket, the upper half showing off his white pajamas with a black diamond pattern. His eyes were half-lidded and he looked miserable. But seeing us, he mostly seemed embarrassed.

"Mr. Keller," he said softly. "Miz, uh…Petersen, isn't it?"

"That's right," Lu said, next to me at his bedside.

I put a hand on the side rail and leaned in a bit. "We just wanted to thank you for everything you did last night."

He looked like he might cry. "I…I didn't do a darn thing."

"Oh, but you did."

He shook his head a little. "I don't remember shooting that man. Just *him* shooting…firing…at me. All the target practice doesn't prepare you. I saw the flame…the muzzle flash… sounded like a damn *whip*…."

"But you kept your head, Ben."

His eyes opened wide and his eyebrows tightened. "I did?"

I nodded firmly. "You did. You fired four rounds off after you got hit."

Now he squinted at me. "That's what they *say* I did."

"That's what you did. That's no small thing."

The angle had him looking up at me; he raised his head to better meet my eyes. "I...Mr. Keller, don't tell anybody. But I don't *remember* doing it."

I was not about to tell anybody.

I said, firm and sympathetic, "It'll come back to you, Ben. It will come back to you. And the part of you where you got shot? The scars you'll heal into? Those'll be your badges of honor."

"They will?"

I put my chin up as if I were about to salute. "Ab-so-fucking-lutely. You will be honored for your quick reaction, Ben. You will, I have no doubt, be presented with the Law Enforcement Medal of Valor. They give those out in Minnesota, you know."

He brightened. "Really?"

I pawed the air. "Oh yes. Be proud. Own this, and stand tall."

"I will, sir. I will." His head was high. Or anyway as high as a guy flat on his back could have his head.

"You look good," I said pleasantly. "Doing well."

"Yes. I'll be out in a few days. Amazing what they can do."

"I'd imagine Clarence Whitlock isn't doing nearly so well."

"Who?"

"Clarence Whitlock. The man you shot. The intruder."

"Oh. Yes. Right. Detective Goedkin did mention that name, but...it didn't stick. He did say the man would likely recover."

"They must have him in Critical Care."

I wasn't relishing having to navigate the hustle and bustle, and patient visitor protocol, of an ICU.

"I believe he's on this floor," Loomis said. "With a police guard on his door."

Lu said to me, "We should be going. Officer Loomis needs his rest."

I gave him a gentle pat on the shoulder. "Miss Petersen here and I will be forever grateful. You saved our lives."

His eyes were slits and his mouth a straight line. "It was my honor, Mr. Keller."

"No. It was your duty. Your honor will be reflected in that Medal of Honor that I know you'll receive."

Lu said, "Thank you, Officer Loomis. Thank you so much."

We went out in the hall and Lu gave me a smirk. "You went over the top there, just a little, didn't you? Kinda oversold that."

I waved it off. "He *wanted* to be sold. He'll have people around here buying him beers for the rest of his days. Now, let's see how the *other* patient is doing."

Past a nurse's station, toward the end of a connecting corridor, a young blond uniformed officer sat outside a room reading a James Patterson novel. Lu and I set up figurative camp at the opposite end of the hall in a modest visitor's lounge area, home to half a dozen overstuffed chairs, a unisex bathroom and a vending machine. I bought myself a Diet Coke and a paper cup of coffee for Lu and we sat and talked over our beverages, Lu still in the black topcoat, me in the fur-collared jacket. It's often cold in a hospital and this was no exception.

"Any ideas," she asked, "about how we get past that cop on the door?"

I nodded toward the nearby restroom. "Start a fire in there maybe?"

"Might work."

"How's that coffee?"

"They may have to pump my stomach," Lu said, making an "*ugh!*" face. She rose and tossed the paper cup sloshingly in a trash receptacle near the vending machine. She looked over her shoulder at me. "I might have an idea."

"Usually a person knows when they have an idea."

"Shut up. I'll be back."

Then, leaving her topcoat on the chair next to me like a skin she'd shed, she disappeared into the nearby elevator, leaving me to contemplate our options, of which we had so far only one: starting a fire in a hospital.

Great.

The foot traffic was minimal—a few visitors, the occasional nurse in blue scrubs or traditional white, sometimes with skirt, sometimes slacks, doctors in lab coats and neck-slung stethoscopes. An intermittent flow. Mostly just me and, way down that hall, that cop reading Patterson.

Where the fuck had she gone?

I found a magazine to pretend to read, a *Time* from two months ago, and wondered if coming around mid-afternoon was such a good idea. Maybe sneaking in, in the middle of the night, would be the ticket.

Then I realized a nurse was standing right in front of me and I reacted with a start.

Took maybe three seconds to process it, but the nurse was Lu, in white, blue-trimmed cap and skirt, her hair ponytailed back the way it had been with Goedkin at my place this morning. She had a zippered gym bag that I gathered contained her street clothes. And she carried a clipboard.

I said, quietly, "I hope you didn't kill anybody to get all that."

"That's quite a conscience you seem to be cultivating."

"I live around here is all. I take it this is that idea you spoke of."

Her nod was crisp and confident. "I talked my way into the nurses' locker room and helped myself to what I needed." She nodded down the hall where the cop sat. "I'll go down there

and tell Brainerd's Finest that there's a personal phone call for
him down at the front desk."

"Front desk, not the nurse's station?"

"If that comes up, I'll say they don't take outside calls there.
And they don't want to disturb the patient by using the room
phone. It's bullshit, but who cares? After you see Dudley Do-
Right get on the elevator, come join me. Or do you like the hospital fire plan better?"

I got to my feet. "I guess once you steal a nurse's uniform,
you've already decided."

"Agreed." She set the gym bag on the chair with her coat.

"But what if somebody sees through your little masquerade?"

She shrugged, utterly unconcerned or at least pretending to
be. "I'm a reporter for the *Brainerd Dispatch* and I was trying
to bluff my way in for an interview with the shooting suspect."

"Jesus. I guess we're doing this."

"No guesswork about it." She raised those sculpted eyebrows, flicked me a little smile, and turned on her heels. Actually
white nursing shoes.

I watched the tall would-be nurse walk with casual confidence down the corridor, glancing at her clipboard now and
then, moving right past the nurse's station and another nurse
coming this direction, and nobody made Lu for anything but
the real thing. Then way down there she was approaching the
cop, who from this distance looked impossibly young, though
an ageless weapon was on his hip. He stood politely and listened. Lu pointed in my direction and he asked a couple of
questions, which she answered, and then he walked toward me
as she slipped into the hospital room.

Unlike the handful of cops on the Sylvan PD, this baby-faced
Brainerd blond was nobody I knew. He did give me a polite
nod before pushing the elevator button, waiting thirty-some

long seconds before the door slid open and the elevator swallowed him without so much as a burp.

I hurried down the corridor, slowing past the nurse's station, where I exchanged some smiles with the women there, and then I was inside the room with Lu and the patient.

He was awake but not alert. Like Officer Loomis, Clarence Whitlock seemed in good shape for a recent gunshot victim. As with Loomis, a single IV fed the patient's needs; and he too wasn't hooked up to a monitor on this non-Critical Care floor, nor was he on a breathing tube.

Unlike Loomis, the bald, trimly bearded Whitlock had his bed cranked up in a near sitting position, both shoulders bandaged, his right more elaborately so. He wore no pajama top, just bottoms—the same white-with-black-diamond pattern as Loomis—and was on top of the covers. Two pillows propped him up further. His right hand was cuffed to the bed's side rail.

Nurse Lu was no one he recognized, nor had he got a look at me last night. An attractive nurse in his room was no cause for alarm, but a stranger in street clothes—not a police uniform or investigator's suit-and-tie—gave him definite pause.

Lu positioned herself by the door, putting an ear to it, cracking it occasionally, keeping track of when the young cop might return to his chair, which should take him a little while, before he realized he'd been summoned by a false alarm.

"Who the fuck are you?" Whitlock asked me.

Not the friendliest individual.

I was at his bedside. I placed my hand on his nearest bandaged shoulder and applied just enough pressure to get his attention. It made the handcuff rattle.

His eyes and nostrils flared. "What the fuck?"

"Quiet or I'll quiet you. I'm Quarry. Does that name mean anything to you?"

He scowled and nodded.

I said, "Just share a little information, and this'll be a short visit."

"About what, asshole?"

Not friendly at all.

"Who hired you?"

"How the hell should I know? That's not how things work, old man. Maybe back in your goddamn day."

"We worked through middlemen. Who's yours?"

"Fuck you!" With his left hand, he grabbed my wrist on the hand that gripped his shoulder and flung it off like an unwanted insect. He began to thrash. He began to yell. *"Help! Medic! Somebody! Get the fuck in here!"*

I tried to settle him down but it was no use.

Lu cracked the door, shut it again. Whispered, "No sign of our cop but some nurses are chatting down the hall. Might be about to head this way."

"Shit," I said.

"Fuck you!" Whitlock said through a big smile. "You are dead, Quarry! Fucking dead!"

"Nurses still talking," Lu said quietly, an ear to the door.

I snatched one of the pillows from behind him and said, "Who is your broker? Where does he work out of?"

"Fuck you! Fuck you!"

I pressed the pillow over his face and pushed him back into the remaining pillow. He kept thrashing, his cuffed right hand making percussive accompaniment and, for a while, he was yelling into the pillow I was smothering him with. The yelling finally stopped. The thrashing, too.

Takes a long time to kill a man that way.

Almost four minutes.

EIGHT

As we stepped into the hospital hallway, Lu said, "So much for you having to live around here."

I shrugged. "People die in hospitals every day."

Our coats and the gym bag with Lu's street clothes had been left on a chair in the little lounge area at the other end of the corridor. We were retrieving them when the young blond uniformed cop stepped off the elevator.

Lu and I exchanged frowns but the cop didn't notice us off to his left as he wheeled to his right, heading past the nurse's station and on to the waiting chair outside the room where Whitlock permanently slumbered. The cop filled the chair and returned to his Patterson novel, a mildly irritated expression the only sign of the wild goose chase we'd sent him on.

We had the elevator to ourselves as we rode down.

Lu said, "They'll know Whitlock was smothered, of course."

She was referring to the reddening of the eyes that was a tip-off to suffocation as cause of death.

"Maybe," I said, zipping up my jacket. "But his eyes were bloodshot already. And don't forget—our detective friend suspected some accomplice might drop by during visiting hours to tie off a loose end."

"Never a bad practice," she admitted, nodding, shrugging into her topcoat.

I added, "And, anyway, why would we come to mind?"

The elevator emptied us into the high-ceilinged modern lobby, underpopulated at the moment. We headed out into the cold late afternoon air and started across the parking lot.

"Well," she said, answering my question, though it had been intended as rhetorical, "Officer Loomis knows we were here today. So we *could* get on Detective Goedkin's radar."

"We could," I admitted.

Her frown grew thoughtful. "And if Goedkin comes looking for us to question, we won't be home. He *did* tell us not to leave the area."

"Can't be helped. We'll deal with him when the time comes."

"Let's try not to kill a cop."

"Do my best."

We were in the Lexus, pulling out of the lot, when she said, "We could wait it out a while at your place. See if Goedkin shows. And if he seems convinced our presence at the hospital was a coincidence, and goes away, we take off to Naperville then."

We'd planned to leave immediately from the hospital; her getaway bag and a suitcase of mine were in the trunk, including extra changes of clothes, half a dozen handguns, two boxes of ammunition, and my shaving kit.

"No," I said. "Every minute we waste puts Susan at more risk."

She drew in a breath. Let it out.

"Agreed," she said.

We were starting out at a little after three P.M. with—even factoring in a restroom break and maybe some food—an eight-hour trip ahead. Taking 94 put us on a perpendicular path, picking up 90 at the Wisconsin Dells. We had an overcast cold day that, when it turned to night, wouldn't benefit from the full moon, the cloud cover blizzard-white and just as blanketing.

At least an hour passed without us sharing a word. I was driving and I thought Lu might nap, but she didn't. I was conscious of her occasionally stealing a look at me. The sky was gray now and the roadside a dirty white. We had the radio on the Oldies station that she seemed to prefer and which I didn't mind. Late '60s up through early '80s.

"One Way or Another," Debbie Harry was singing.

Outside Minneapolis, night already settling in, with me still behind the wheel, Lu said, "You're not very talkative."

Her eyes were on the road with the lights of the city up ahead. The dashboard bathed her in ghostly green.

"You mean in general," I said, "or right now?"

She looked at me now, casual. "I wouldn't call you generally *un*-talkative. You don't usually seem to mind carrying on a conversation."

That didn't require a response.

The almond eyes narrowed on me. "Did it bother you back there?"

"When that truck went around us and cut in too close?"

"No. At the hospital. Suffocating that bastard."

I flicked a frown at her. "Why should it? He was just some lowlife killer-for-hire."

"Right. Hired to kill *you,* so fair is fair."

I was looking at the road. "Right."

"But it threw you a little, didn't it?"

"Yeah. Can't you see? I'm a mess."

My eyes weren't on her directly, but I caught her little smile just the same. "You don't like wet work up close, do you, Quarry?"

"Let it go."

Her arms were folded. "You were a sniper, weren't you? In the war. You were protected."

That earned her a glare. "Protected? What, by Artillery? You think a 155-millimeter shell knows which tree to avoid?"

"You like a little distance. You like your homicides abstract."

I turned the radio up. Eric Clapton was in the middle of "I Shot the Sheriff."

She worked her voice up over it. "Nothing to be ashamed of. You're human. I like that in a man."

Irritation furrowed my brow. "Do I look like I feel ashamed?"

She studied me momentarily, then said, "Troubled. A little troubled."

"My daughter was kidnapped. Somebody might have already killed her. Okay?"

"You didn't raise her."

"Huh?"

"You didn't know she existed till she was over forty, so don't feed me that sentimental slop. Oh, I think you care about her, and want to save her and all that jazz. But I don't like to see you feeling guilty…"

"Guilty!"

"Feeling uncomfortable doing what you did…what you had to do…back at the hospital. Seemed like it took forever."

"Not long. Less than five minutes."

"Not long. Just an eternity." She turned toward me, straining her seat belt. "Look, people like us wither away if we retire. It's good you're back in the game. Biggest mistake I ever made was dying. Nice to feel alive again, isn't it? Not that you're happy your daughter getting grabbed initiated your comeback. And we're gonna do our best to retrieve her. I'm here for you. Always had a soft spot for you, Quarry."

My irritation faded and I let some air out and, finally, smiled at her, a little. "I love you, too, Lu. When we get past Minneapolis, you can take the wheel a while. And I can drive *you* bug-fuck with personal questions."

"You won't get jack shit for answers!" she said with a laugh.

And for a long while that was it for conversation, at least conversation that didn't have to do with restroom and food and fuel breaks.

We were just outside of Madison, with Lu at the wheel, when

my cell phone trilled. The phone ID said BRAINERD PD. I answered it.

"I'm sorry to bother you this time of evening, Mr. Keller." Goedkin sounded even wearier than this morning. It was a quarter to nine P.M. He'd had a long day, but hadn't we all.

"Not a problem, Detective," I said. "I was going to call you first thing tomorrow."

"I stopped at your place, Mr. Keller, and have been calling your landline. I'm glad to finally get hold of you."

"I should have let you know immediately, Detective, but Louise and I took off to see her sister for a couple of days. Millie's in Madison and we're almost there." Should somebody's GPS start wondering. "I apologize because you said we shouldn't leave the area, but when her big sis heard Louise was visiting from Billings, she talked us into a visit. We'll be back in a few days."

The pause was long enough for the connection to crackle.

"Do check in as soon as soon you get back," Goedkin said.

"We'll absolutely do that. Is there a problem?"

"Officer Loomis said you were nice enough to stop by his room and wish him well. Did you happen to drop in on our other wounded individual? Mr. Whitlock?"

"Gracious no," I said. "Why would I do that? If I did, I'd give him a piece of my mind."

"It's a little late for that. He was murdered this afternoon."

"Oh dear. Somebody just walked in and, what? Shot him?"

"No. He was smothered to death. With a pillow."

"Goodness. I wouldn't wish that on anybody."

"You didn't happen to see anyone suspicious lurking around the third floor at the hospital?"

"No one lurking at all. Seemed quiet. Who could have done this? One of those accomplices you speculated about?"

"That's our starting point. But do check in when you get back, Mr. Keller. Sorry to bother you."

He clicked off and I clicked off.

Lu was looking at me. " 'Oh dear'? 'Goodness'?"

"Well, we're polite here in the Midwest."

Grinning now. "You'd've given Whitlock a piece of your mind, huh? Can you spare it?"

Then we both laughed for a while, though I think we both knew I really had gone a little over the top again. But Goedkin seemed to buy it. I did take the precaution of tossing the phone in a snowbank at a Madison rest stop. Lu had a cell and I could always pick up a burner.

I took over driving and Lu had a nap. She knew the Chicago area better than me, so I'd make sure she was driving when we got close.

The Chicago sector's killing-for-hire broker resided in a castle lacking only a moat, and yet like many French Provincial estates it retained an absurdly inappropriate element of quaint country cottage. Situated in Green Acres—a wealthy patch of Naperville north of 75th Street east of Route 59 that had nothing to do with Eddie Albert and Eva Gabor—Wallace Conlon's home with its sloping roofs, high arched windows, conical towers, and gray-stone facade made shacks out of its million-dollar neighbors.

Neither walled-in nor gated, the mansion on the banks of the DuPage River enjoyed half an acre of land to itself, a world and minutes away from downtown Naperville. We left the Lexus parked a block away on the street, having already geared up with a shoulder-holstered gun for me (my reliable Browning nine mil) and Lu's .38 revolver, snugged down in a coat pocket. We were both all in black, me again in fur-collared black leather jacket, her in Duval's black topcoat, looking like actors in a Spaghetti Western who wandered off the set.

Lu had her hand gripping the revolver in that coat pocket, but I was keeping my hands free. We had done no surveillance and could not be sure what security we might encounter. From her last visit here three years ago, when a confab of Midwest brokers was held, she recalled that Conlon at the time had a couple of former military guys on staff as security. She also remembered the layout of the house—she'd stayed camped out in one of the mansion's many bedrooms for a couple of days when that conference was held—and had drawn me a diagram of each of the three floors as she remembered them at the Rodeside Grill when we stopped outside Madison.

The mansion's eight-thousand square feet of living space sported six bedrooms with bath, a two-story foyer, a cavernous great room, formal dining room, kitchen with double islands, family room, office/library, lower-level rec room, and indoor swimming pool. Cozy little pad.

"*One* guy lives there?" I'd asked, across from her in a booth in the pine-paneled, aggressively outdoorsy restaurant. Behind us, a stuffed mountain lion on a mini-cliff was growling down at a stuffed bear coming after him.

"Just one," she confirmed. "He's had three young wives over the last forty years. The first died under suspicious circumstances. The second two settled for generous pre-nups."

"No children? No little grandchildren running around cute as killer bees?"

"Nope. He's handsome in his boyish way, though. Between wives he was never short of company."

Since Lu stayed with him for a few days, maybe she'd been one of that company. Not my business.

I asked, "What about that security team?"

"Two are always on duty. Armed. Like I said, ex-military."

"Any guard dogs?"

"No."

"Any electronic shit?"

"Not when I was there last, no."

"Will we have to kill the guards, you think?"

Her shrug could not have been more casual. "Let's try not to. I have handcuff zip ties in my getaway bag. Also duct tape, everybody's gag of preference."

"What *don't* you have in your getaway bag? It's Batman's friggin' utility belt."

She smiled wickedly. "I'm still alive, aren't I?"

"Don't brag. So am I, and I'm older than you."

At the mansion in Green Acres, past a circular drive, we hid in the bushes facing the house, among some tall bare trees that provided a Snow White-in-the-spooky-forest effect. I don't scare that easily, though…except when the first security guard showed himself.

In a black baseball cap, he was six-two and had linebacker shoulders, his big frame—not in any way fat—stuffed into a black windbreaker (really too lightweight for the weather, but not restricting his movements the way anything heavier might). It said SECURITY over his right windbreaker pocket and on his back it said

SECURITY,

like he wasn't kidding the fuck around. The holstered weapon on his hip implied the same damn thing. So did his smooth oval of a face, which had no noticeable lines in it, as if he hadn't used it much for either smiling or frowning.

He came around back of the house in an easy stride, a flashlight in his left hand, its beam stroking the grounds, including our bushes, where right now we were ducking way down. He moved slow but steady, like the Earp brothers and Doc Holliday on their way to that vacant lot near the O.K. Corral.

When he had passed us, Lu—as we'd planned—emerged from the bushes without him seeing, though he did hear something and turned. She froze, as if frightened (maybe she was) and he walked toward her and positioned himself before this female intruder like the Colossus of Rhodes.

"This is private property," he said. "You need to leave right now."

Her tone was just friendly enough. "I'm an old crony of your boss. I was here for the conference during Covid—were you working then?"

His chin lifted. He looked down at her. "I remember you now. Why didn't you call ahead?"

"I did. He's expecting me."

"I wasn't told."

He was reaching for the walkie on his other hip when I whacked him over the back of the head with the barrel of the Browning. He staggered like a tree thinking about falling, then I hit him again.

He fell face down and Lu was on him like he was a bronc she was riding, pulling his arms back and zip-tying his wrists with the plastic cuffs. Then she got duct tape from her topcoat pocket, ripped off a sizeable piece, and slapped it tight over his mouth. He wasn't feeling a thing.

We were wearing driving gloves, by the way, which I'd provided. Fingerprints.

We searched him, left his wallet and took his sidearm, a Heckler & Koch .45, an accurate, reliable low-recoil weapon. He knew his shit, our sleeping beauty.

It took us both to drag him by the ankles into the bushes;

when we got him hidden away, we borrowed his belt to secure his ankles. If you think he might make it to his feet when he came around, and hop somewhere, not likely. He might even be dead or dying. Two blows like I delivered can do that.

What we did next was a tad risky.

We went in the front door, using keys we collected from the guard. We found ourselves in a ballroom-size foyer that rose all three stories, with a sweeping staircase inviting us upstairs. But we didn't go. Lu led me through a formal dining room into the kitchen, a stainless-steel wonderland of appliances and reflective surfaces, and stopped at a door that her shared intel told me was the security guys' room, which she described as an oversize closet.

She opened the door fast and I went in the same way, and, rising from a chair at a small table, a Black guy with no shirt on and just his black chino trousers turned and looked at me indignantly. And why wouldn't he? I was some old guy intruding and he had pectoralis muscles and abs that would have intimidated Schwarzenegger in his heyday.

But I had a Browning nine mil and told him to turn around. He didn't like it, he didn't do it right away, but goddamnit, old guy or not, that was a gun, so he turned around. He had muscles on his back that I never saw on a human before.

Still, he also had the same delicate skull we all do, and I whammed the barrel sideways into the back of his head; he, too, staggered and required a second love tap before introducing him to the floor, face down.

Lu helped me drag him over to a sofa and laid him on his belly, face turned to the right. Some '80s action movie set in Vietnam was on a modest flat screen. The limited space didn't include an elaborate set-up—a refrigerator, a john, a small table by a comfy old chair and that sofa, all very secondhand-looking for a joint like this. But what the hell? This was just for the help.

In case he was sandbagging it, I kept the nine mil trained on him while Lu zip-tied his hands behind him and then she used his belt on his ankles. The back of his head was pretty bloody, but he was breathing, for now.

We looked upstairs in the bedrooms, each of which had a fireplace, and didn't find our unaware host. Nor was he in the elaborate library, where the walls were of leather-bound books, the kind nobody reads, and the furniture was leather-upholstered, the kind nobody but the boss sits on.

Lu was frustrated for a moment, when we ran out of bedrooms; but then she smiled and nodded. "I know where he is. I know."

The indoor pool, like the foyer, had to itself an echoey chamber that again rose the full three stories, the side walls a stylishly distressed tan brick, a full wall of windows—three rows of four—providing a view onto the terraced back yard down to the river, shimmering in refracted moonlight. The pool itself was probably thirty-five feet by eighteen, its blue triangle generously notched at the right lower corner to make room for a hot tub. I was a swimmer and it made me envy this prick, and I'm not one to be that way.

He was small, much too small to be living in such a big house. He was, as advertised, handsome, but also entirely hairless and pudgy without being fat, like a big baby, and shouldn't have been able to attract three beautiful young wives no matter how much money he had. But of course that was wrong. There wasn't a horrible male who couldn't find some lovely female willing to suck his dick if the price was right.

I had been lucky in my lifetime to know a number of women who couldn't be bought by the likes of this oversized fetus in a black Speedo, terry-cloth half-robe, and mesh swim shoes. He had a small table next to him. Folded open was another James Patterson novel. And yet I couldn't get in the fucking airports.

He also had a bottle of The Singleton of Dufftown 54 Year Old Single Malt Scotch Whisky on that table with a snifter a third filled with the golden liquid. If you're wondering, a bottle of this alcoholic nectar went for over forty grand. You heard me.

He was leaning back in a Timber reclining beach chair. I had one in the fitness center at the lodge. Went for maybe $140. No forty-grand models were available, so he made do.

It was hot and humid in there and Lu slipped out of the top-coat, revealing her black jumpsuit, which was still too warm for this chamber. She tossed the coat on a lounge chair on the other side of the table and I tossed my jacket over hers, revealing my black sweatshirt-and-jeans ninja ensemble. Our host—no longer unawares—was sitting up, with no back support from the recliner. His mouth hung open, his eyes popped and he flew to his sandaled feet.

His initial shock gone, he summoned a smile.

"Lu!" His voice was a tenor that went with his baby-ish physique. "Lu, Jesus Christ, Lu! You're *alive.*"

She seemed unimpressed by his enthusiasm. "Come on, Wally. You had to suspect I was just paying somebody to write me out of the script."

"I guess I hoped so. Who's this?"

He was looking at me like she'd brought the gardener in with her.

"Somebody you've heard of," she said. "But never met."

"Oh?"

I joined the conversation. "My real name isn't important. But my broker…to me *the* Broker…called me Quarry."

He was already plenty pale but he got paler. "You're famous

in some circles, aren't you? You turned on your own kind and that wasn't nice."

"We were never in a nice business, Mr. Conlon, were we? Can we skip straight to why Lu and I knocked out your security guards and tied them up like Christmas geese?"

He tasted his tongue. Didn't like it as much as that forty-grand Scotch apparently. "I didn't figure you walked right in and made yourself at home. I do take certain security measures. I'm a man of means, after all."

"King of the Road?"

He didn't get it or at least didn't react. "What can I do for you, Quarry? Lu and I are old friends. More than just business acquaintances."

I didn't want to think about that. For just a second I realized she might have been delivering me to this pudgy prick.

"I think you know why I'm here," I said. "A guy calling himself Duval, now making a new home at the bottom of a gravel pit, was likely one of yours. And then another asshole, name of Whitlock, came around to finish the job. I smothered him with a pillow this afternoon in the hospital where he was recovering from two bullets I put in him."

His face stayed impassive but his eyes flared. "Not my people. I swear. Maybe there's a broker in Minneapolis who Lu could take you to, to—"

"I don't think so. I think it's you. What you may or may not know is this: a woman, a true-crime writer you might have heard of since you read airport shit, was snatched either by your people or whoever hired this done. What you may not know is that this woman is my daughter."

He batted that away. "I don't know anything about it, not anything. I swear to you, Quarry. Kidnapping is not on my playlist."

"But you know who hired the hit on me. That you do know."

Now his nostrils flared, too. "I don't! It came in through a middleman. We're buffered to the hilt these days, Quarry. Wholly insulated. There are layers upon layers."

I showed him the endless black hole that was the tip of the nine millimeter. "Not good enough. Try again."

His fat little hands came up and patty-caked the air. "All I know is where it emanated from. That's all I know. Some little podunk town."

"What little podunk town?"

"Some Iowa bump in the road.

"*What* Iowa bump in the road?"

"...Port City. That's all I can tell you. That's all I know."

It was enough.

So I'd come full circle. Back to where I'd broken from the Broker. Back to where I'd met Peg Baker. Back to where my daughter's life began. But why? And this son of a bitch didn't seem to know.

Lu came over and grabbed him by a baby arm and dragged him to the edge of the pool.

"Convince me," she said, and shoved him in. The splash was considerable and she was already dripping when she knelt at poolside and thrust in her clad arms and fished out a pudgy pale arm and dragged him glug-glug-glugging to the surface; water trickled and drizzled down his bald head onto his face like he was an apple pulled from a Halloween bobbing barrel.

"I don't know! I swear I don't!"

She dunked him.

Brought him up after maybe a minute. It felt longer, like when I smothered that asshole at the hospital.

"I don't! I don't know! I don't!"

She dunked him longer this time. Held his head down with both hands.

Brought him up and his eyes were open but they weren't seeing anything. And he had nothing to say.

She let go of him and after a few seconds he was floating face down, like a turd in a punch bowl.

"He got me wet," she said, brushing off irritatedly.

"Not sexually, I hope."

That made her laugh but it was on the hysterical side. Her hair was black tendrils. Her eyes were wild.

"I thought he was a friend," I said to her, getting a towel from next to where our dead host had been sitting.

She dried herself off some. Said, "Not a bestie."

I shrugged. "Who was it said, never too late to tie off a loose end?"

She tossed the towel. "I hope you never think of me that way."

"Same back at ya," I said.

NINE

As Lu drove, I used her cell phone to call ahead to the Hampton Inn & Suites in Bolingbrook, to see if a room was available; one was.

The dashboard lights continued to bathe us in ghostly green. Traffic on the freeway at this post-midnight hour on a weeknight was relatively light, the landscape a gray thing under low cloud cover, though icy sparkles glimmered in roadside snow accumulation. Somehow it was as if we were moving through a world where only we were real and everything, everyone else, an illusion.

The silence, but for the engine purr and tire hum (we'd tired of the Oldies station), began to feel oppressive. Lu was lost in thought and so was I, but neither of us had turned any of that into words.

Finally I asked, "What the hell could make someone in Susan's homey hometown hire her murder?"

Lu didn't reply; she had an exit to take.

Turning onto Remington Boulevard, she said, "We don't know that anyone hired her murder. She's presumably still alive. Someone hired *your* murder. And someone—someone else?—kidnapped her."

I winced, trying to make sense of it. "Hired her kidnapping? Hired it through Conlon?"

"Could have."

"No, I think he'd have copped to it."

Her mouth flinched in the otherwise impassive face. Hands tight on the wheel, she said, "Say what you were thinking—I screwed up."

"I wasn't thinking that."

"I held him under too long. Shit. I meant to ask him a few more questions."

Shrugging, I said, "You just wanted him to take you seriously. And he should have. It got away from you, a little. These things happen."

"Thanks for saying so, anyway." Her face swung toward me for a moment, highlighted by dashboard green. "But why take Susan?"

I opened my hands. "My little girl's a true crime writer. A somewhat famous one, who was researching an unsolved crime or crimes. That much I gathered from her."

"So *what* crime or crimes? And again—in Port fucking City? Really? Aren't there a dozen innocent reasons, having nothing to do with her research, that could take her home? In which case, what could've stirred up the need for somebody to grab her, not to mention hire a hit on her father? What, did she run into a bitter old beau at a class reunion, wanting revenge for not getting a little after the prom?"

My laugh was more a grunt. "Is that the best we can come up with?"

"Seems to be....Here's the motel..."

We pulled into the Hampton lot; less than half an hour ago we'd been in Naperville. A twenty-buck bribe to the desk clerk got us into the business center after hours.

We were pretty wasted after that eight-hour car ride from Brainerd to Naperville, not to mention our assault on an unfriendly mansion and the mess we left behind. But those words Port City, Iowa, were burning in my brain and Lu understood. She had a smart phone we could have used to look things up, but having a normal-sized computer screen to share would be much better.

I had a credit card with a phony name but a real account—which I'd also used to check in—that bought us the time we needed to fund an Internet search.

With our two chairs pulled up to the one computer, and Lu positioned at the keyboard, we just stared at the blank screen in numb exhaustion, not exactly sure where to start.

Finally Lu, in the search box, typed in: *Port City, Iowa.* She glanced at me and I leaned over and typed another word next to those: *Murder.*

Up popped a dozen articles from the *Port City Journal,* a dozen more in the *Quad City Times,* and four from the *Des Moines Register.* To read any articles in full we had to pay the freight. I used my credit card to buy web subscriptions to all three publications, again with my real card and fake persona.

We read all of it, which took about an hour, although we skipped much of the *Times* coverage because the *Journal* was a sister paper and the articles were retreads, except for one covering a Davenport killing that went into more detail.

Three murders were spread out over five years—attractive young women, each dumped outdoors during the winter in a park. Either by happenstance or cunning, the killings occurred in variant though adjacent law enforcement jurisdictions—one body discovered in Weed Park in Port City itself, another at nearby Wild Cat Den (a state recreation area), and the most recent in Davenport's West Lake campgrounds.

The young women had all been recent high school grads who were still in town, either going to community college or planning their next move. They were good students and popular at Port City High, with one thing in common: they'd been cheerleaders. Pictures of them in their cheerleading togs accompanied many of the articles, providing tragic cheesecake.

After the third killing, the media had started calling them

the Cheerleader Murders, which is what presumably prompted the likes of true-crime writer Susan Breedlove—mentioned in several newspaper articles—to look into the unsolved, probably related crimes. She had some coverage as a visiting celebrity in the *Journal* and the *Times*.

"She was in Port City," I said, "poking around, not long before she came to spend Christmas with me."

Lu nodded. "Probably drove straight from Port City to Sylvan Lake. This must be the project she was in the middle of."

I was able to sign onto Susan's e-mail account and we found only one message that seemed pertinent—Deputy Chief Clement Maynard of the Port City Police, whose name turned up in numerous of the newspaper articles we'd just read. He was responding favorably to Susan's request for a follow-up interview on her current book in progress, and their meeting was to be at the police station...tomorrow afternoon.

Finally we went to bed.

The room's walls were pale green but for the brown one that the king-size bed's headboard was backed up to. You've probably stayed at a Hampton Inn, so fill the rest in for yourself.

With everything we'd done today, and with everything we'd just stuffed into our heads about three unsolved homicides in the Port City area, we might well have tossed and turned; we might have talked deep into the night. We might even have fucked our way into post-coital slumber.

But we were just too damn tired for any of that and anyway sleep came quick, though Lu's trademark sort of cute snoring beat me to the punch.

I arose at sunrise, which was around seven, and took a quick shower. Lu was still sleeping. I put on my swimsuit—like Karl

Malden used to say, never leave home without it—and a hotel robe and my running shoes. I left my roommate a note on the nightstand, saying I was going down for a swim.

Many times at a motel, a swimmer like me runs into little kids cavorting. That's what little kids do and I get it, but I prefer no noise and privacy. I got lucky. No kids splashing and screaming and echoing, not even a businessman, cavorting or otherwise, were present. I had the whole place to myself. The walls were blue, the drop ceiling a little low for my tastes, the pool itself taking up most of the space. The brown-tiled decking around the rectangle of water was narrow but did accommodate a few chairs and tables, all metallic, with a hot tub separate from the pool itself.

I didn't have a mansion to put around it, but otherwise this was perfect. For one thing, no dead guy was floating face down. I did my laps, about twenty-five—I often logged fifty when I was younger—and climbed out, toweled off, and slipped into the hot tub. I'd been in there about three minutes when Lu in a hotel robe came in, tossed a rolled towel on a chair nearby, dumped the robe and revealed a black swimsuit, one-piece but hiding no mysteries, then toe-tested the hot tub water and joined me.

We leaned against the sides across from each other.

She had her hair pinned up and no makeup on, a very different look for her. But still astonishingly attractive.

"That pool at Conlon's got your juices going," she said.

"Not really. If I'm at a motel, I always swim. I swim daily at the lodge fitness center back home, and love every second."

"Well, good for you. I work out at a health club in Billings and I hate every minute of it."

That made me smile. "The next step is, obviously, heading to Port City. You aren't known there, so that shouldn't be a problem. We can figure this out in the car, but if you have any second thoughts…?"

"Are you going to insult me again?"

"No. But this is getting a little hairy. We're leaving a trail of corpses behind us like Bonnie and Clyde on a bad day."

"All the more reason for us to play this out. Now. We need to decide how we're going in. I can be a researcher working with Susan. I have business cards in the name Lila Anderson that say Freelance Journalist, Boulder, Colorado, with my cell number."

"What's my role? Two researchers doesn't make sense."

"You're right. We'll stay close to reality—you're Susan Breed-love's biological father with whom she recently connected. You're concerned that she's dropped out of sight, working on a dangerous case. You bumped into me and we decided to join forces."

I nodded, fine with all of that. "So am I Jack Keller from Sylvan Lake?"

"No. Using your Sylvan Lake name and situation might backfire on you. We don't know what we're going to run into, or what we're going to have to do."

I nodded, her point well taken. "I have several other I.D.'s along. I don't want to use the one I checked in with here, since there's a chance, slight maybe, but a chance that it could link us to our surprise Naperville visit."

She nodded. "And I'll just be a true-crime writer's researcher, accompanied by the concerned parent of the possible next victim."

"That's right. But we need to keep one thing in mind."

"Which is what?"

"What happened to the last true-crime writer who had an appointment in Port City."

✻

Forty years hadn't changed Port City much except in pre-
dictable ways. We took Interstate 80 through a mix of farmland
and the occasional small community until at our left emerged
the edge of the Quad Cities. At the outskirts of Davenport,
where the businesses ran to convenience stores and RV lots, we
took Highway 61 over rolling Grant Wood farmland corrupted
by the likes of John Deere sales, a drag strip, and meat peddled
out of the back of a roadside trailer truck.

As a hill leveled out, the town of twenty-five thousand
announced itself by way of fast food, Wal-Mart and car dealer-
ships. Turning left onto Park Drive, a commercial stretch continued, though the mall was clearly dead or dying. But people
still had to eat, and in addition to McDonald's and the usual suspects were Mexican joints, diner-style restaurants, and Chinese
fare.

My memory of Port City was two hills with much of it in the
valley between, and that held sway: you can change demo-
graphics but, short of acts of God, geography stays the same.
East Hill—where we'd come in—was the same old mix of commercial and residential while West Hill remained home to the
fading mansions of nineteenth-century logging and pearl
button tycoons, fortunes made thanks to the town bordering
the Mississippi River.

I was behind the wheel, taking us to the all-way stop at the
end of Park Avenue, then turning down steep River Drive past
a suspension bridge that indicated the rickety affair I'd come in
on decades ago was a distant memory. A manufacturing hub
gave way to a modest downtown that appeared to be thriving
as long as tattoo parlors and pawnshops were your idea of
progress.

Where River Drive flattened out, I cut through a world of

warehouses and swung left up to Fifth Street, past a sprawling grocery and drug store called (I kid you not, as Jack Parr used to say) DRUG TOWN. Continuing through the intersection of Fifth and Mulberry took me past a VFW Hall on my left that had been there back when, still cater-corner from a three-story tenement where I'd done surveillance on the last hit I'd done for the Broker. At street level was a Mexican restaurant/ bodega; next to it down the block stood a squat building that had been a taxi stand where my partner Boyd got himself into trouble. My late partner Boyd.

On Fifth Street, the police station, which hadn't been there forty years ago, occupied with the fire department a low-slung modern brick building devoid of any noticeable personality. It sprang from where a residential district turned commercial, sharing a corner with a dead gas station, an accountant's office, and the sprawling convenience store with gas pumps that had likely killed its competition.

We parked in the PD lot and went around front and in through double glass doors. The small waiting area was dominated by a row of mismatched chairs, a humming vending machine, and a dying rubber plant. Behind a Plexiglas window a navy-blue-uniformed female was working a dispatcher's console. We had to wait a while before she could give us her attention.

"Two o'clock appointment with Deputy Chief Maynard," Lu said to the woman, who had a head of curly blond hair, dark-framed eyeglasses, and a put-upon attitude.

"His appointment is with Susan Breedlove," the dispatcher said. "You aren't her."

"No, I'm her researcher. I'm filling in."

"It's ten after two o'clock now."

"We came a distance. We're here now. I hope we haven't caused the deputy chief any inconvenience."

"Do you have identification?"

"Yes, but as I say, I'm not Susan Breedlove."

"I know....Who *are* you?"

"Her associate, Lila Anderson." Lu had a card ready and handed it through the hole in the Plexiglas.

The woman studied it like a tiny eye chart, then handed it back.

"I'll tell him you're here," the dispatcher said. "But he may not see you. You aren't Susan Breedlove."

"Yes, we've established that."

The dispatcher got on the phone, turning away for privacy.

I said to Lu, "Who's on first?"

Lu said pleasantly, "Shut up."

Soon we were sent down a hallway of cold institutional concrete block walls broken up by the occasional closed door and decorated with ancient framed photos of ancient cops looking like the security team at the Overlook Hotel. The dispatcher had told us we'd find Deputy Chief Clement Maynard on the right, the last doorway down.

But he met us in the hall, a big, broad-shouldered man in his late forties, his hair short and sandy and thinning, eyes light blue, features chiseled right down to a square, trimly bearded jaw. In his dark blue uniform with the usual badges, patches and name tag, he looked formidable but friendly.

"Ms. Anderson," he said, his voice a husky baritone, his smile white against the sandy beard. He extended his hand and he and Lu shook. "Pleased to meet you. I haven't heard from Ms. Breedlove and was getting worried. And who's this?"

Lu gestured to me. "This is Susan's father, John Jamison."

"Mr. Jamison," he said. "You have a talented daughter. You must be proud."

"I am. Call me 'Jack.'"

We shook hands. His grip tried just hard enough.

"Please," he said, gesturing toward the doorway, stepping aside.

Once we were all within the long narrow space, he got into the swivel chair behind a big wooden desk with its computer and neatly arranged stacks of folders and printouts. The rest of the room was taken up by a conference table beyond which were four smaller desks, metallic, with chairs and computers and stacks of work. Like Brainerd, Port City looked to have a small detective staff. Filing cabinets hugged the side walls under a few framed modern pictures of officers in uniform and an array of plaques and awards. No other officer was present.

Two wooden chairs were waiting for us opposite him and we took them.

"Would you like coffee or a soft drink?" he asked. "We don't have a secretary but I can ask the dispatcher to—"

"No thanks," Lu said. "We're already on her bad side."

He grinned. "Everyone's on Clara's bad side."

I said, "Maybe it's because somebody named her 'Clara.'"

He chuckled and asked, "When can we expect Ms. Breedlove to arrive?"

I said, "We hoped you might have heard from her. She hasn't been answering her cell phone or her landline. We came through Davenport and stopped at her house and she isn't home. No sign of her car either."

Lu said, "Do you think we should be concerned?"

He folded his hands and leaned forward. "Do you have *reason* to be concerned? We could file a missing persons report."

Lu frowned. "Don't we have to wait forty-eight hours?"

Maynard waved that off. "That's just in the movies and TV. But you do need circumstances that suggest the individual is missing. Is it like her to drop out of sight suddenly?"

"Actually, it is. She may be following a lead." Lu sighed. "Susan's a single woman with few ties. She can up and go anywhere at any time and not tell a soul."

"Well," Maynard said, "she's been investigating a multiple murder inquiry. Who knows what she might have encountered? Perhaps…well, we'll keep that option open for now. What is it I can do for you?"

Lu said, "Susan has only just brought me in, and I was counting on her to bring me up to speed. I've read the media accounts—so has Jack. I just know there've been three murders of young women over a five-year period, with enough similarities to suggest a serial killer may be the perpetrator. I'm hoping you can fill us in on whatever you've come up with."

Maynard shook his head glumly. "I've only met with Ms. Breedlove in a preliminary way," he said. "I shared with her what I know, but most of that has been what you've seen in the media."

I asked, "Has the reporting been accurate?"

"Yes. If you've read the news stories, there's little more I can tell you." He unfolded his hands and flattened them on the desktop. "It's a tragic damn situation. These were popular girls …homecoming queen candidates in their high school days. Cheerleaders, too, which of course the media loves. They were above-average students—two were attending our community college, the other planned on enrolling in nursing school in the Quad Cities, after saving some money. All three lived here in Port City, though as you probably know from what you've read, their bodies were discovered in three different jurisdictions."

"But all," I said, "in this area. A local park, your Wild Cat Den, and a Davenport campgrounds."

He had started nodding before I finished. "That's correct," he said. "And that obviously complicates matters. We've put together an informal inter-departmental task force, but what we can do is limited."

Lu said, "If you're looking at serial killings, have you called the FBI? My understanding is three homicides are enough to bring them in."

"We tried," Maynard said with a disgusted grimace. "And the killings share some haunting similar characteristics. The bodies were all found in parks, for example. The similar age of the young women, their shared blonde hair color, that they'd all been high school cheerleaders...plus one more commonality that we have withheld from the media, which I am hesitant to share even with you. And, then, there are other quite different characteristics, major dissimilarities, a few also withheld from the media, which is why it's been difficult to convince the FBI to send in a team."

Lu asked, "Can you share those?"

"One of the young women was found fully clothed. One in a sheer nightie. Another, naked. The causes of death were in the media. You'll recall one victim was killed by a blow to the head, probably with a hammer. Another had her throat cut. Another was strangled."

"It sounds to me," I said, "like somebody is fucking with you."

The harsh language didn't faze him. He said, "I would agree. The jurisdictional ploy. The clothing disparity. The murder methods."

Lu asked, "Do you have any suspects?"

Maynard drew in a deep breath, then dispensed it in a sigh. "We have one. We have a very good one. Christopher Andrew Lowe. He's the son of deceased wealthy parents. Wild as a kid, sent off to military school to avoid juvie, but supposedly straightened out. He runs the family's trucking business with his cousin."

He slid a file folder across to Lu. "It's in here with copies of the crime scene photos and evidence reports. I didn't give these to you."

I asked, "Is the withheld evidence in there?"

"No. It's redacted."

Lu said, "Then why don't you tell us. We won't go public with it without your okay."

He thought about it. Thought about it for what seemed an eternity. Probably about as long as it took Conlon to drown.

"All three girls were pregnant," Maynard said.

TEN

What Port City called South End was a largely rundown area of lower-middle-class housing and a stretch of Highway 61 heading out of town where an attempt had been made to create a restaurant and retail section by way of metal stud-frame commercial buildings. That well-meaning effort had so far not been able to overcome the stench of the nearby feed company plant that poured gray smoke into the air twenty-four seven.

Past the city limits was the Island, a wide, flat plain of around thirty-thousand acres whose sandy soil for a century had flooded too often for crops to thrive. Over the next hundred years, though, that soil had lent itself to growing musk and watermelons, and roadside stands thrived here during the season. So did a few hardy businesses, some year-round, including Lowe Trucking, whose president—Christopher Andrew Lowe—was a person of interest in the so-called Cheerleader Murders.

According to Deputy Chief of Police Maynard, that status as the "almost" key suspect was diminished by alibis from Lowe's cousin Jason in all three cases as well as their person of interest declining to be swabbed for DNA, which without an arrest he was not required to do. That frustrated law enforcement, as the most current murder—just a little over a month ago—had given up the genetic calling card of the father of Victim Number #3's unborn child.

That DNA had not provided a match in any national databases. Christopher Andrew Lowe had never been arrested for anything, even ducking reform school by enrolling in a military academy.

The previous two victims had both been cremated, as the serial nature of the killings hadn't become apparent until the third murder. Number #1 (Weed Park) had seemed a one-off, Number #2 (Wild Cat Den) had been outside of Port City PD's jurisdiction as had Number #3 (Davenport's West Lake campgrounds). All the Port City PD had on their person of interest was a rumored reputation for womanizing (two wives had left him), and that Lowe's only alibi came from a family member. Also the fact that Victim #2 had worked at the family-owned trucking firm…despite Christopher Lowe's status as a prominent pillar of the community, president of one of Port City's most thriving, job-generating businesses.

With Lu at the wheel of her Lexus, we rolled into a vast crushed-rock parking lot where rows of trucks crowded the horizon: semi-trailers, flatbeds, step decks, dry vans, box trucks, tankers, you name it. A cement apron around the small yet formidable office building fronting the place provided visitor parking, empty till we filled a slot.

The building was a many windowed two-story tan brick affair with a three-story facade; the windows didn't reveal anything and seemed mostly for show in what might have been a recently constructed branch bank. This was not the rambling glorified greasy garage I'd expected.

It was mid-afternoon. Several hours earlier, we had checked into the Best Western Inn on the other side of the world and taken time only to freshen up and get into something that didn't look like a ninja costume on Halloween. I shook out my sport coat and put on a tie and chinos, Lu got into a baby-blue silk blouse and flared black pants and heels. Presentable, we headed out for an appointment we hadn't made.

We were buzzed in, but nobody asked us who we were. Inside, a wide stairway awaited that took us up to a shallow but impressive lobby, dominated by a facing trophy cabinet of physical awards, framed photos, and toy trucks bearing the company logo. The newness of the facility was obvious from the flat pastel painted walls and fresh-looking handsome wood trim everywhere with occasional fieldstone flourishes, lending the place an upscale look.

Our anonymous entry got us a greeting from a clean-cut guy who emerged from behind the trophy case wall. In a black sweatshirt (again with company logo) and jeans, he nonetheless had a professional demeanor, friendly but wary. He was about my size and, pushing forty, sported a slimly muscular build and a boyish face offset by dark hair going steel gray.

"Jason Lowe," he said by way of introduction. "Help you folks?"

"Lila Anderson," Lu said, with an easy smile, extending her hand to be shook, which he did, though his expression said he was half-expecting a joy buzzer. "And this is John Jamison. I'm Susan Breedlove's research associate and Mr. Jamison is her father."

"Oh?" he said, his smile as his blue eyes came to me not entirely masking a continuing wariness.

"We've lost touch with Ms. Breedlove," Lu said. "She's dropped out of sight. We're combining some research into the case she's looking into…Susan's a true-crime journalist, as you may know…and hope to find out what's become of her."

"That sounds a little ominous," he said.

I said, pleasantly, "Not necessarily. Susan can get side-tracked when she's digging into a subject. So we haven't placed a missing persons report or anything. So far we're just trying to connect with her."

His hands went to his hips, an unconscious Superman pose. He was casually businesslike as he said, "Ms. Breedlove was here about a week and a half, two weeks ago. I'm not sure exactly what day. We work long hours here and things can get a bit blurred."

"Understood," I said. "She was with me for Christmas, so it would've been before that. A few days ago she headed home, which is Davenport...no sign of her there...and since then she's sort of dropped off the grid."

"Well, I hope it's nothing serious."

When we made no move to leave, he frowned and gestured to a doorway onto a hallway that cut horizontally through the building. "Let's take this to my office."

He led the way past closed doors at the left and, at right, a bullpen of dispatchers at computers and office workers also at their screens, in cubicles that stopped at about their shoulder level, giving their bullpen an open feel. Most were women, under forty, who flashed smiles as we passed. We might be prospective clients, after all.

At the end of the hall was a big glassed-in office. An expensive mahogany desk with beautifully carved touches sat center-stage on a hardwood floor, pastel walls again set off by handsome wood trim; behind the desk was a display cabinet of more framed awards and photos of local, state and even national dignitaries. Big framed photos of Lowe Trucking in its various stages since the 1940s rode the walls proudly, including a shot of two middle-aged men in suits and ties and smiles, each with a hand on the other's shoulder. A small round conference table with chairs was at the left; they were of the same mahogany as the desk. A globe was nearby.

Today Port City. Tomorrow the world!

Our reluctant host paused before the glassed-in enclosure as if it were a shrine. "This was my uncle's office," he said. "He and his brother Clarence founded the company. It's Chris's now."

Lu said, "Your cousin Chris."

"Yes. My first cousin Chris—he's president of the firm, ever since Dad and Uncle Clarence died in a small plane crash, ten years ago. I'm executive vice president, by title, but kind of chief cook and bottle washer in practice.... My office is right here."

This proved to be next door, around the corner; Jason's workspace was about half the size of his cousin's, uncluttered but for a metal desk sharing a computer screen with piles of hard copy and folders. Again, the history of the trucking firm was reflected in framed photos on the wall, black-and-white yesterdays and color todays.

Two customer chairs were opposite the desk, which he got behind, and we took ours while he took his.

"This is quite an operation you have here," I said.

He perked up. "Yes, and it's growing. I hate to say so, but Covid was a boon to us. Our business boomed, and it still is."

A double-size window onto the lot provided a view of activity —semis being driven into the adjacent service building, trucks pulling out of the huge lot, as well as the rows of other varieties of transport vehicle awaiting their turn to hit the road.

Lu asked him, "Family business?"

"Yes. My dad and uncle were melon farmers who thought having a little sideline would be a good idea. And it grew into this. A hundred-plus trucks and seventeen acres."

"Never any doubt you'd get involved?" I said.

"Oh, plenty," he said with a mild smile. "I was going to be an architect. Planning to start college when 9/11 happened. Kind of turned me around. I did two tours in Iraq, came home, Dad and Uncle Clarence were taken from us, and Chris and I stepped in."

"What branch of service?" I asked.

"Marines."

"Semper fi, Mac."

That got a genuine grin out of him. "Not the same war, I'm guessing."

"No. But there's always *some* war, isn't there?"

"Never a shortage." He shifted in his chair. "Listen, I'm sorry you missed Chris." He said this to Lu. To me, he said, "That's who your daughter talked to. She and Chris spoke for, oh, half an hour. Surprised it took that long."

I asked, "Why's that?"

Irritation made his face seem less boyish. "Well, this whole 'Cheerleader' business…the police from all around here are focused on one stupid thing."

Lu asked, "Which is?"

"Rebecca Edwards. The second girl they found? She worked here, out in the office. Just a summer job, saving up for college."

Like Jason here, she never made it.

"Excuse me for asking," Lu said bluntly, "but was your cousin involved with her away from work?"

"Hell no," he said, the blue eyes flaring. "Doesn't matter who you are, we have strict guidelines on fraternization. Has to be aboveboard and entirely mutual. Our HR person doesn't put up with any nonsense."

I said, "We had a conversation with Deputy Chief Maynard."

He stiffened, just a little. "Did you."

"Chief Maynard indicated your cousin has a reputation as a womanizer."

No friendly smile now. "Chris had a couple of marriages break up. That kind of thing always generates talk."

"Maynard also said Chris was wild as a kid. Had to be shipped off to military school."

His shrug was dismissive. "I had the same kind of reputation. And I went to military school, too, and it really straightened me out. Prepared me for what was up ahead."

"Did it straighten your *cousin* out?"

He sighed. "We're two different people, Mr. Jamison. I get grease under my fingernails. Chris gets manicures. I make sure the wheels are rolling, he keeps the business growing. He's in Chicago today, working on purchasing a small competitive firm. We're expanding."

Lu asked, "Will he be back today?"

"He's staying over. Be back tomorrow."

"Will you be seeing him tonight?"

"No, we pretty much see enough of each other at work. I live nearby. Christopher's in town. Could I set up an appointment for you? In the afternoon?"

"That would be great."

He put us down for one o'clock tomorrow and then walked us out, again past a row of smiling employees. Seemed like a great place to work.

As we walked through the expansive parking lot, our feet stirred gravel.

I asked, "So, then—you were with him, the nights all three girls were killed?"

"That's right."

"Just you two?"

A nod. "Just us two. We get together once a week and watch movies. He's got a great setup, giant screen, theater sound. We do sometimes argue about what to watch."

We were at the Lexus. "Oh?"

"I like comedies, Adam Sandler, John Candy. He likes Chuck Norris and Steven Seagal. If there's one thing I can't stand..." He made a face. "...it's war movies."

We went directly—or as directly as possible—from South End to West Hill, to do a little recon on the home of Christopher Andrew Lowe.

"Home," however, was understating it—this was one of those aging mansions overlooking the Mississippi, dating to the 1800s; but at some point within the last thirty years or so the big white two-and-a-half-story rectangular structure had been refurbished. The place had the unadorned look of a school or hospital out of that robber-baron Gilded Age, dressed up with money-green shutters and sheltered behind a gray picket fence and trees and shrubbery.

Snugged back behind a row of more ostentatious dwellings, Christopher Lowe's house—almost certainly the family home— was divided from its neighbors by an alley. An unattached two-story garage, designed to match the mansion, had been obviously built many decades later; to the left of the garage, a brick walk wound past more shrubs and trees up a gentle slope to the front entry. The basement shutters showed enough of that lower floor to require a wrought-iron staircase up to the entry door.

We couldn't get a better look without getting out of the car and having a walk around the place, and attracting undue attention from neighbors.

So by late afternoon we were in a cozy corner booth at an Italian restaurant called Salvatore's in downtown Port City— early enough that we had the place to ourselves. I suggested we eat light because we had something to do this evening. I didn't have to tell Lu what that something was: Christopher Lowe wouldn't be at his home tonight, which meant we could be.

Waiting for an order of lasagna to come for us to split, sipping glasses of Moscato—best be no refills with what lay ahead—I got into it.

"Susan may already be dead," I said.

"Possible," Lu said, with a touch of doubt for my benefit.

"Maybe *more* than possible—could be probable."

Even with the eatery empty but for the occasional waiter, I kept my voice low—nice and intimate.

"There are reasons to keep her alive," Lu insisted. "Whoever did this, whether Chris Lowe or some other bastard, may feel he can't get rid of her before finding out what she knows."

I nodded. "And what she might've passed along."

"To anybody, *everybody* she might have talked to. So that's what you have in mind, isn't it? To see if she's being held in Christopher Lowe's mansion?"

"Well, with him not home, what better time to find out?"

She sipped wine. "Have you retained your breaking-and-entering skills in your dotage?"

I shrugged. "Should be a simple pick-and-hit."

Various Italian crooners on the sound system were shielding our conversation—Dean Martin, right now.

"Before all this, I hadn't done that kind of thing," she said with a sigh, "in a very long time."

"I haven't done it much lately myself. But there isn't much to it. We've already ascertained Lowe likely goes in the front door atop those wrought-iron stairs. Up which we'll go, and I'll just pick the lock. Standard residential, a credit card should do. Using picks, under thirty seconds. Deadbolt, could take a couple minutes to pick. Go right in."

She raised an eyebrow. "And set the alarm beeping and counting down for thirty seconds, during which time you better find that fucking keypad box."

I waved that off. "The alarm box is usually on the wall by the entry door or in a closet close by, and either way, I just smash it with a hammer. Home security systems don't alert the police until the countdown has run out and the alarm siren is going off....Here's our food."

After the meal, I stopped at the Menard's near the Best

Western Inn and bought a ball-peen hammer. In our room, I got out of my shoes and took a nap. Lu watched TV with the volume thoughtfully low. If I slept past two A.M., her instructions were to wake me.

But I woke up a little after one A.M., took a cold shower, got into my black sweatshirt and black jeans and black running shoes. Lu had already changed into her black jumpsuit.

Ninja time again.

But no guns. If we would happen to get caught in the act, firearms would bump the charge up from breaking and entering to armed robbery. We could risk my driving gloves and one of Lu's pairs of latex gloves, and that was it. With my daughter a missing journalist investigating a notorious local serial killing, I might be able to talk us out of getting charged at all...*if* we went in unarmed.

We parked a block away from Lowe's, one street up. The big white box had a number of its shutters open wide enough to create glowing stripes on various windows. The master of the house had left an assortment of lights on around the place, perhaps to make it seem like somebody was home. Windows on the two-story garage indicated one vehicle present—a sports car under a tarp, the other stall empty. So we wouldn't have to use flashlights and risk a strobe effect being picked up on by neighbors. We could turn lights on and off around the mansion without much if any worry.

Going in was a piece of cake: credit card indeed opened the front door, with the alarm box to the right on the wall past the entry way. Two slams of the ball peen shut off the warning beeping.

We prowled the house together, taking it a floor at a time, in what might otherwise have seemed a disorganized fashion. We would check a room where the lights had been left on, then shut them off and go on to another room and find a wall switch or a lamp to turn on. We did not want the place lit up in an attention-attracting way.

Going through the main and upper floors of the place took over an hour. We found no sign of Susan or any of the dead girls, either; oddly, we also found no rooms that looked very lived in. Maybe Lowe had an overzealous housekeeper.

The kitchen had the expected array of gleaming appliances, high-end cabinetry, and marble countertops, but only minimal food and drink in the stainless-steel slab of a fridge. The pastel-green-walled living room offered an impressive view of the river through a picture window, the furniture expensive in a blandly modern way, with only the original wood trim to indicate the age of the edifice. Two first-floor bathrooms and a guest bedroom were well-appointed in a similarly blah manner. The master bedroom, where the pastel colors gave way to masculine browns, had a walk-in closet that was damn near empty but for a few plastic-bagged suits.

Lu and I frowned at each other.

"It's as if," she said, "he doesn't live here at all."

The finished basement, however, told a different story.

This floor was one big room but for doors onto a bathroom (arrayed with men's grooming products), the furnace area, a door onto a patio, and a possible storage space with a Yale lock. The living area, carpet-tiled in shades of gray, had a pool table centerstage, a big double bed with black silk sheets and a leopard-pattern comforter extending from one wall, facing a media cabinet with a big flat-screen TV and shelving of audiophile gear, high-mounted speakers all around. The semi-underground chamber's walls were painted black, the closed shutters on windows making it seem like permanent night.

Another, smaller stainless-steel refrigerator held various

goodies—wine, beer, cheese, cold cuts, and frozen dinners, with a microwave on a short counter above which was a cupboard of boxed microwave meals. One wall bore pictures of framed team-autographed posters of University of Iowa football schedules going back years (Lowe was apparently a benefactor). Another wall bore photographic posters of women with lots of hair and teeth and lipsticked lips and bikinis and surgically enhanced breasts.

It was a little boy's idea of a bachelor pad.

The upstairs remained the domain of the two wives that had left him, their ghosts haunting that world, though it had been stripped of any sign of them beyond that kitchen and the furniture. Down here, the business exec could bring somebody else's wife, or daughter, and play Hugh Hefner.

"Doesn't he know," Lu asked, almond eyes getting as wide as they could, "*Playboy* stopped publishing?"

I shrugged, adding, "*Penthouse* is still around. And *Hustler*.... I want to see what's behind that door."

My assumption that it led to a storage area suddenly seemed doubtful.

"Actually," I admitted, "I don't, but..."

Her hand settled on my shoulder. "You need to."

I picked the Yale lock and the door opened onto darkness, a dark black that conveyed a chill beyond the winter outside.

My fingers found a wall switch.

If the adjacent room was Hef's dream pad, this was the Marquis de Sade's playroom. Not a big area, just a red-walled square as if a one-car garage had been cut in half.

From hooks mounted on the scarlet wall at left dangled gags, chains, shackles, whips. Against the far wall was an X of wood large enough for a human to stand and be cuffed at the wrists and ankles. At right, waiting for when they might be selected

and dragged into position, were benches and stocks. Against
the left rear wall was a black-metal cabinet that rose almost to
the black-tiled drop ceiling with six drawers containing God
knew what—leather and bondage gear? A metal dog dish with
maybe a quarter inch of water in it was near the wooden cross.

"Christ," I said. "Is this where Susan's been kept?"

"I don't know," Lu said, "but she's not here now."

ELEVEN

Next morning, we slept in.

Another long yesterday had got the best of us, me in partic-ular. All we had lined up was that appointment at one P.M. with the boss at Lowe Trucking, so we could afford to log a little sack time.

Since Lu and I would again be presenting ourselves as a dogged researcher and worried father respectively, I put on my sports coat and tie and some chinos while Lu made herself look professional in a pale yellow silk blouse and tan slacks, her hair pulled back in a ponytail.

We took the Bypass to South End where we swung in for a late breakfast at a restaurant called Bunny's. It startled me slightly, because Bunny's had seemingly changed very little—a single-story dark-wood building on a small rise surrounded by a big parking lot that separated it from a pizza place on one side and a laundromat on the other. You'd think things would have changed in forty years.

They had. The interior, once two rooms (restaurant and bar) was one big space now and the patrons were blue-collar types, including a few families. A diner vibe was reflected by a wall of window booths opposite a counter with a kitchen pass-through, and between them a scattering of tables where pancakes seemed the dominant entrée.

Just inside the door was a framed 16" by 20" color picture of Peg Baker in her *Playboy* Bunny costume, wielding a round tray of drinks; she was easily ten years younger than her daughter in this shot, which had been published in the magazine. She was all the corn-fed blonde pulchritude a man of any age could ask for. A little plaque on the frame under the busty smiling image said, OUR FOUNDER — PEG BAKER, with the year of her birth and of her passing.

I paused there, transfixed, memory making my dick twitch, while we waited to be seated by a fiftyish portly hostess who was not wearing a Bunny outfit.

Lu was watching me.

"That's her, huh? Susan's mother?"

I nodded.

Lu commented, "Living doll."

Not anymore.

We settled across from each other in a booth. Once again, an interior decorator assigned a diner had gone nuts with a red-white-and-blue theme broken up a bit by reproduction signs advertising Coca-Cola, Sunbeam Bread, Kit Kat candy bars and assorted other all-American goodness.

Any morning rush was over and the booths to our immediate backs were empty, with no filled tables nearby. As long as we kept our voices down—with the awful country-western on the sound system to further mask us—we could talk freely over our post-breakfast coffee (for her) and iced tea (for me).

"All three girls," Lu said, stirring cream into her coffee, "pregnant? What do you make of that?"

I shrugged, sipped the tea; pretty good—brewed. "I'd say we're dealing with a sociopathic cock hound."

A sculpted eyebrow rose above an almond eye; her full lips twitched a smile. "Ah. My least favorite type of psychotic. But how did you come to make that diagnosis, doctor?"

I sipped iced tea, thought for a few moments, then said, "He has his fun for a while. This isn't Ted Bundy talking a girl into his car for a one-way ride. This is somebody who has an affair with a young woman long enough to get her knocked up. Then knocks her off."

Lu shivered. And it took a lot to get that kind of reaction out of her. "Jesus. Had to kill them, huh? Couldn't just spring for a goddamn abortion."

I flipped a hand. "The threat of a forced marriage or bad publicity must have been too much."

"Or," she said, "he's just a sick fuck."

"Or," I said with a shrug, "he's just a sick fuck."

She smirked. "Possibly the kind that has a homemade S & M dungeon off his rec room."

"Yeah. That kind. Which is the good news."

"What's good about it?"

"We almost certainly have our killer in Christopher Lowe." I sighed; not something I do that much. "But what has he done with Susan?"

Lu's cell phone trilled and she answered it. "...Yes, this is Lila....Good morning, Jason."

She put the phone on the tabletop between us and we both leaned in and listened to the Lowe cousin we'd met.

"We're going to have to push that meeting with Chris till tomorrow," Jason Lowe said. "He's got his hands full, I'm afraid."

"Oh?"

"Chris came home from Chicago about half an hour ago and found his house had been broken into. The alarm box smashed to pieces. He's waiting at home for Deputy Chief Maynard and a few detectives to come and take their photos and prints and such. Can we just say tomorrow at the same time? One o'clock?"

"That'll be fine," Lu said pleasantly. "Your cousin's probably lucky he wasn't home. Some of these break-in artists can get violent."

"That's right. Chris can take care of himself pretty well, but yeah, that's right. Sorry for the inconvenience!"

"Not at all," Lu said.

She thanked him, retrieved the phone and clicked off.

"Well," she said.

I was shaking my head. "Probably my fault. I figured our trucking magnate, with a four-hour drive back from Chicago and a one P.M. appointment waiting, would go straight to his office."

"So what now?"

Maynard had given us contact info on Sheriff Frank Sloat and Davenport PD Detective Harold Reeves, who were heading up investigations into the Wild Cat Den and West Lake campgrounds murders.

"Support our local sheriff," I said.

The county jail, which included the sheriff's office, was a modern two-story dark-brick-and-glass rectangle separated by an alley from the Public Safety Building, which was where we'd met with Deputy Chief Maynard yesterday. Just inside were several rows of airport-style seating, accommodating a scattering of sad, unsavory family members awaiting their turn with incarcerated loved ones who were not here to take a flight.

The glassed-in sheriff's office was to the right, a surprisingly small affair with two females in the outer area—a dispatcher and receptionist. We had called ahead and the sheriff knew we were coming—he had spoken to Susan about the case several weeks ago and was sorry to hear she'd gone missing.

Soon we were sitting across from a fleshy yet haggard-looking walrus-mustached individual who sagged within his crisp light tan shirt with its gleaming gold badge, khaki epaulettes and matching tie. His square, unadorned desk was as orderly as he wasn't, the computer screen on the desk seeming to stare him down. So did the faces on a bulletin board of wanted posters.

The bulletin board hung crooked as did a modest array of framed public service citations. The most impressive award was a bowling trophy atop a filing cabinet.

"We didn't know we were dealing with a possible serial murder situation," Sheriff Frank Sloat said in a weary, husky voice that went well with his baggy eyes and a haircut that may have come courtesy of a jailhouse barber. "Ours was the first death, three years ago, at Wild Cat Den."

I nodded. "A state park."

"Yes. But there are limited visitors during the winter. Over the decades, in this corner of the world, there have been occasional other homicides out at the Den, most resulting in arrests and convictions. So they're unrelated to this current crime. We're talking killings that go back to before World War Two, while the most recent prior to this one was in the Vietnam years. Both perpetrators were veterans of those conflicts."

War can fuck some people up.

"This first murder," I said, "did not take place in your jurisdiction."

"That's correct. Wild Cat Den is over four-hundred acres of State Park…sandstone bluffs, rock formations, and all sorts of trails. But it's mostly a summer and fall kind of place. That's when it's colorful. In winter it has a bleak, lonely kind of beauty that doesn't attract many. Not even a ranger on duty that time of year. Just not enough to do."

I leaned forward. "Deputy Chief Maynard said one of the victims was clothed, another in a nightie, another naked."

His nod took effort. "Ours was clothed. The second girl was in a, what are they called, teddy. The other, naked. That's one of the differences in M.O. that has kept the feds out of this thing so far."

"Which doesn't make sense," I said. "That's a pattern, going from clothed to nightie to nude."

"I agree, but the feds didn't. When the second girl turned up dead here in town, in Weed Park, about a year later, we did start talking serial killing, but in a kind of…'Jesus, what if this is a serial killer?' way. But as you know, there were enough differences between the first two homicides to keep the FBI out. This thing may get on their radar now—three is the magic number."

"Magic number?" Lu asked with a frown.

"Takes three kills for the FBI to classify homicides as serial killing." Sloat opened a folder on his desk and, before pushing it our way, said pointedly to Lu, "These are not for publication, but you can have a look. This is the first girl."

She was blonde and on her back, wearing a short gray knit sweater dress, shapely but that shapeliness was twisted, her legs askew, her long hair spread like seaweed. She lay near brown, almost black skeletal trees on a bed of snow like a gift under a Christmas tree.

"This is the second," the sheriff said.

We looked at crime scene photographs of another young blonde, her body in the wispy teddy just a pile of former humanity but the ghost of beauty still haunting her. She lay on her right side on a bare patch of snowy earth near a rock formation.

"And number three," he said.

The third dead former cheerleader was again dumped in a pile of snow near some leafless foliage. She was naked. On her stomach, head to one side, hair flowing. Another gift under the tree. But unwrapped this time.

I asked, "No suggestive forensic evidence at all?"

Sloat shook his head. "Not to speak of. Well…maybe one thing, and it relates to the lack of forensic evidence. The young women's bodies…" He gave Lu a sharp look. "…and this is not for publication at this point, Ms. Anderson…appear to have been washed, that is, bathed before being dumped outdoors, whether naked or put into her clothes. Or perhaps put *back* into her clothes."

Lu said, "This does sound like a serial killer, and a smart one. Wash away any evidence."

His melting-wax expression was right in there with the saddest I've ever seen. "Ms. Anderson, we deal with lots of things around here. Robbery, hit and run, child abuse, rape, and yes, homicide. But this kind of cold-blooded behavior is nothing we've encountered before. You have a man who has had relations with a woman, been most probably in a relation-*ship* with a woman, with a pregnancy resulting…and yet he can kill that woman, wash her naked body, and strip her like he's cleaning a fish, or dress her up like she's a plaything? It's like something out of a horror show."

Like the kind of horror show that might have gone on in Lowe's basement S & M playroom.

"Mr. Jamison," the sheriff said, "I hope you're able to track your daughter down soon. Not to be an alarmist, but her inquiries could have stirred up this madman who is somewhere among us. I hope I'm wrong."

"Susan has a will of her own," I said. "She may just be off on some investigative trail and I'll hear from her when I least expect it."

Not a lonely trail at Wild Cat Den, I hoped.

He stood behind the desk. His smile was a ghastly thing.

"I'm hopeful that my colleagues on these other departments," he said, "Deputy Chief Maynard and Detective Reeves up in Davenport, have enough now to convince the FBI to come in and, frankly, really do the things that none of us is qualified to do... Is there anything else?"

There wasn't.

The Davenport Police Department—on Harrison Street on a wide one-way at the edge of downtown—was housed in a facility with the same kind of rectangular, intersecting shapes as its Port City counterpart; but three times the size, the brick of its brick-and-glass outer walls a light tan. It might have been a school. Certainly lessons were taught there.

The detectives in the bullpen were all in uniform, dark-blue with silver badges reflecting fluorescent light. Again, we'd called ahead and the beefy Black cop who met us offered up a smile that didn't have much to do with smiling, and shook our hands in a perfunctory manner, a rather soft handshake that had better things to do than waste energy.

Detective Harold Reeves led us into an interview room, as if we were suspects, and took an end seat with Lu and me facing each other across the bare expanse of processed polished wood.

"Since you've spoken to Sheriff Sloat and Deputy Chief Maynard," he said, his voice as resonant as it was quietly irritated, "you know everything I do. We haven't held back from each other, my colleagues and I."

"And yet," I said, "you haven't been allowed to form a task force and really dig into this thing."

His nod was slow motion. "That's true. But as I told Ms. Breedlove—and I cooperated with her as fully as I felt I could, when she came around—the FBI seems poised to finally take this on. And they are much better equipped to handle what seem to be serial killings."

"My daughter is missing. You're aware of that."

"I am."

"And Ms. Anderson is her researcher."

"I'm aware of that."

"So you understand anything you can share with us would be appreciated."

Lu added, "And would remain confidential till you give us the okay."

His face was a blank mask. "I'll tell you what I *can* share with you. This is a dangerous situation. Involving a dangerous individual, whoever he is. You two are in over your heads. The FBI will soon be on its way, now that it's become evident that this really is a serial killer we're dealing with."

"The differences in the M.O.," I said, "are what discouraged them till now."

He flicked the air like a bug was bothering him. "That's right. But to my eye, frankly, the similarities outweigh the differences."

Lu said, "I would agree. Do you have any suspects? Or at least persons of interest?"

"Not that I can share with you."

I said, "What about Christopher Lowe? He's at least a person of interest. One of the victims worked for him, and he's a notorious local womanizer, right? Who has refused to be swabbed for DNA?"

"If you think," Reeves said tightly, "that I am going to share every phase of this investigation with you, the way Sheriff Sloat did, you are sadly mistaken. I don't appreciate amateurs messing around in my backyard."

"Ms. Anderson here is a professional," I said, surprised by how pissed-off it made me, having Susan denigrated, "and my daughter is a best-selling journalist and true-crime author. Call me an amateur if you like, but it's my fucking blood that's gone missing."

A tiny sneer. "That kind of language proves you aren't professional."

I got to my feet. "Well, if you and Sloat and Maynard were professional, you wouldn't have to call in the federal troops to bail your asses out. What you're dealing with is a killer who's eating his cake and having it too—getting his rocks off killing these girls even as he knows he's confusing the issue by varying the method of kills."

The Black cop studied me.

Then he said, "What's your line of work, Mr. Jamison?"

"Retired."

"What was your line of work?"

"Insurance investigator."

And I had the phony business card to prove it.

"Before I talk to you again," Reeves said, "I need to see some real I.D. Some proof you're the missing woman's father. And I'd like you, Ms. Anderson, to demonstrate that you are who and what you say you are. Because something about you two smells."

We got out of there fast. No smart comeback, just a glare from both of us. And a toothy smile from him.

In the Lexus, with me at the wheel this time, I said, "That's why I try never to deal with cops. I could write a treatise on the dangers of getting involved with cops."

We sat in silence, each going over mentally what we'd learned, and hadn't learned. Just outside the city, we were approaching the exit to Highway 22. She pointed.

"Let's take the scenic route."

"No thanks."

"Why?"

"Not in the mood."

What's the opposite of sentimental? Not far from Davenport on 22, part of the Great River Road, was the vast, yawning rock quarry that the Broker had named me for in his dry sarcastic way. It was also where I'd killed him. A long time ago.

"My daughter," I said, heading back to Port City on Highway 61, "is an attractive young woman."

"I'm sure. But not that young. Around forty, isn't she?"

"Yeah. But she was a cheerleader in high school, she told me. And she's blonde."

TWELVE

Port City had no shortage of Mexican restaurants or Mexicans either. The biggest industry in town was a Heinz plant, from where the catsup you last used may well have come. In the mid-1950s, migrant workers who picked the plant's tomatoes began to take root here. Now many worked indoors year-round.

I pulled the Lexus into the parking lot of Las Lomas on East Hill, not far from the Best Western Inn. Dusk was tinting the yellow adobe-style restaurant a cool blue under a low-hanging gray sky. In a rustic wooden booth, Lu and I shared fajitas. The all-Hispanic staff was friendly and efficient.

We spoke little. Our efforts over these last two days in Port City had been focused, but the possibility of Susan still being alive lessened by the hour. By the minute. Add to that the possibility an FBI Behavioral Analysis Unit could march into town at any moment—agents who would not be as easily rolled over by glibness and fake ID as these small-town cops were. We had to move fast.

But neither of us knew what our next move was.

"We could talk to the parents of the dead girls," Lu said over an after-dinner margarita (I was having Diet Coke). "That's about all that's left."

"We already *know* who did this," I said.

Lu nodded. "Christopher Lowe. Quarry, we haven't even met the son of a bitch yet."

"It's time to get acquainted."

She frowned, the almond eyes slitting. "And what? Squeeze it out of him, where Susan is?"

Yes, I hated torturing people. But.

"We may not have any choice," I said.

Dusk had given way to night when we got back to the Best Western Inn, leaving the Lexus in the under-occupied parking lot at the rear of the building where the lighting could have been better. Only five cars (one of them ours) and a panel truck were back here. The smoky gray cloud cover was turning the moon into a blurry button and the stars into nothing at all. Didn't seem to be many lodgers at the motel tonight. This was that dead week between Christmas and New Year's, and Port City was not exactly the average vacationer's idea of a good time.

We were on the third of three floors toward the end of the hall, near an exit, as I'd requested. Lu used her key card, pushed the door open, and paused in the doorway to reach her hand around to click the light switch. She didn't get that far because a big black shape reached out a big white hand and yanked her into a darkness that should have told me at once that someone was waiting—I'd left a reading lamp on and the pitch black should have alerted me.

It hadn't, and now I was the one in the doorway fumbling for the light switch, and I got grabbed by the arm by someone I couldn't see, a second someone who couldn't have been the shape that had snagged Lu and tossed her like a rag doll near the double bed, almost giving her a soft landing but providing the floor instead.

The door slammed behind me and somebody, not me, turned on a light in the open bathroom; that provided enough illumination for the two hulking figures to keep track of us as one started whamming fists into me and the other returned to Lu lying still on the floor, in a posture that eerily recalled the first dead girl photo.

Once I could have mixed it up with this guy—not that I was a master of martial arts or bare-knuckle boxing or anything, but I'd been able to handle myself. Only now I was a year past seventy, a survivor of open-heart surgery, and I was fucked. I felt a helplessness wash over me and I didn't like it one bit. I was just this thing on the floor getting pummeled, like bread dough being prepped for an oven.

The gunshot wasn't all that audible—it was silenced but made that distinctive cough, louder than you'd think but still not really loud. What *was* loud was the yelp of the other guy, who'd gone over to check on Lu. He was on the floor, on his back like an upended bug, both hands clutching his sneakered right foot, with blood squirting through his fingers in little shimmering scarlet ribbons.

Lu was standing over him, the arcs of black hair swinging, strands of it flying as if trying to escape her scalp, her almond eyes bugging, her lovely mouth smiling down in self-satisfied ugliness at the screaming brute she'd just shot in the shoe.

This all happened in a flash, and the big guy who'd been pounding on me turned toward his companion's yelp and I flat-of-my-shoe kicked him in the ass. He went flying into a small round table and was just getting up when I snatched the lamp from that selfsame table—the lamp I should have remembered I'd left on before leaving earlier—and cracked its base over his skull in a shower of heavy glass and shut his lights off.

Lu was kneeling over her fallen assailant, training on him my silenced automatic—which had been under my pillow, where she'd snatched it from in the fuss—but he seemed beyond caring, busy wailing in pain and crying, clutching his foot in red wet hands.

They were both men who had to weigh around two-thirty, Lu's Hispanic and bearded, mine white and bald, whether by nature or a razor, I couldn't say. They wore jeans and the

Hispanic was in a red-and-black plaid shirt and the white guy was in a green-and-black plaid shirt, like a couple of mismatched lumberjacks.

I didn't figure them for lumberjacks, though. Nor the typical thug. But I felt confident I knew what they did for a living.

Lu took command, nodding toward the open bathroom door, saying, "Get me a hand towel."

I did.

She handed me my silenced nine mil and pried the bleeding guy's hands off his foot, which she wrapped with the black towel, knotting it around.

"You may never tap dance again," she told her patient, who was whimpering, looking up at her like a child who'd been slapped by Mommy.

Then she said to me, "There's duct tape in my getaway bag. Secure the other fucker."

I did that, marveling again at the Batman's utility belt nature of that bag. I secured my guy's wrists in front—in back is better, but it's more conspicuous—and his ankles. Another slash went across his mouth; it would come off nasty, as he had a beard. Every male asshole these days wanted to be a goddamn mountain man.

"We'll get you help," she said to her charge, "but we're in no hurry. Better face it—you've got a footful of fucked-up metatarsals. But don't worry. Four or five months of P.T. and you'll be fine. Skin graft or two, bone graft, you'll have the spring back in your step in no time."

His beard was getting wet from his tears. She and I helped him up to his feet. Getting them out of there was slow going, what with one shot in the foot and the other bound at the ankles. But we took our time in the stairwell near our room. Duct Tape Boy I let lead the way, a couple of steps ahead of us, with my Browning on his back. Duct Dynasty hopped on his one good foot with his hands secured in front of him like an altar boy. Both had their yaps duct-taped shut.

We did not encounter anyone in that stairwell, nor in the rear parking lot, where the panel truck turned out to be theirs. You will not believe this, but it's true: on the side of the truck was painted the Lowe Trucking logo and the company's address and phone number. They had been parked toward the back, between two cars, and I stupidly hadn't made that.

We made them climb awkwardly into the back of the panel truck. I got behind the wheel—a key fob had been on Duct Tape Boy—and Lu followed in the Lexus. It was about twenty minutes to get from one side of town to the other.

Mid-evening now, several lights were on in the basement and the first floor of the big white rectangular house with the money-green shutters and gray picket fence. The trees in the front yard that hid the mansion from its neighbors most of the year were turning to spidery filagree in winter.

Duct Tape Boy went up the winding walk to the short flight of stairs with their black-wrought-iron railing, and Duct Dynasty did his hop hop hop thing and waited for us and our guns (Lu had her own by now) on the front stoop.

I rang the bell.

Waited.

Lu and I exchanged looks. The two men were looking at each other in disgust and dismay. With themselves, I'd imagine.

I rang it again.

Finally the door cracked open and a narrow face, trimly bearded—not ZZ Top in the least—looked out to give us a wary eye, as if he were thinking, "Whatever could these two scruffy truckers and this old guy and mature babe be doing on my front porch?"

I pushed Duct Dynasty in, using him to open the door wider, and our unwilling host followed it back. Lu nudged her sniveling, moaning he-man in the spine with her gun and he went on his own steam, if propelled by the weapon's snout.

The smashed alarm system box was just as we'd left it, though the pieces that had fallen to the floor had been swept away.

"What's the meaning of this?" Christopher Lowe asked indignantly. He was taller than his cousin and several years older, with shortish black hair in a Caesar cut and a tanning-bed tan, and unquestionably handsome features, like Hugh Grant but more so. He was in—Jesus!—a maroon silk dressing gown with black lapels and cuffs; black pajamas, also silk, were under there, his legs said. And he was wearing—god fucking damn!—matching maroon slippers.

"You misplace these clowns?" I asked him, jerking my head toward the two prisoners. Duct Tape Boy with his hands together belonged on a street corner begging. Duct Dynasty looked like he was wearing one scarlet shoe.

Lowe thought about the question.

Then he said, "They drive trucks for me."

"I bet they do," I said. "You have a closet handy?"

"Certainly."

"Does it lock?"

"It does."

I had Lu's roll of duct tape in my jacket pocket—I was in the fur-collared black bomber jacket again—and I wrapped the two men together, back to back, securing their arms good and tight. They were Siamese twins with a real transportation problem. They should hire a truck.

The closet was nearby, hanging with expensive-looking rain- and topcoats, and I stowed the two truckers in there, our host reluctantly locking them in.

Lowe led us to his study, one of the apparently little-used rooms on the upper two floors that we'd seen last night. The chamber was masculine in its dark wood paneling and deep brown leather-upholstered furnishings, and the wall-to-wall volumes gave an impression of literacy, although of course these were leather-bound books-for-show.

I plopped him down on a couch—putting him behind his desk would mean checking the drawers for weapons, and I was in no mood. Lu got us a couple of dark-wood and leather chairs and we sat facing him. We both had guns. Pointing them at him would have been overkill, so we kept them in our laps, casually, at angles that wouldn't hurt anybody including us.

Would take only a millisecond to turn the weapons on him and send him to the hell he so surely deserved.

A silver deco cigarette box—a cigarette box!—was on the end table near where he sat. He asked permission to get himself a smoke and we granted that.

Lowe lit himself up with a matching deco lighter and said, casually, "I would imagine I need to get Juan to a doctor…a discreet one. Did you drop something heavy on his poor toes, or perhaps shoot him in the foot? That would seem redundant, since he's clearly figuratively shot himself in the foot already, by way of failing to do what he was sent to do."

Lu asked, flatly, "Which was?"

"Not *kill* you, certainly," Lowe said. He laughed lightly. It bothered me that he didn't seem at all scared. Oh, he was scared, all right. But, man, could he mask it well.

He added, "When you think me capable of that, you misread me entirely."

"Do we," I said.

"You," he said to Lu, holding his cigarette between a thumb and forefinger and pointing it at her like a tiny gun, "are a researcher for Susan Breedlove, I understand." He turned to me, his eyes slightly hooded and as dark brown as the lush mahogany around us. "And you? You are a concerned parent, Ms. Breedlove having made herself scarce."

I frowned. "Made *herself* scarce?"

"Or," he said, "who can say what's become of her? I have no direct knowledge of that."

There was more sneer in my smile than smile. "Then why did you send your bully boys around?"

Cigarette in hand, he waved that off, creating a smoke trail. "Well, not to kill you. That can be accomplished far more easily than the direct physicality of a beating." He grinned at me— actually grinned. "I would venture to guess that you, in your day, might have been a real handful."

"Ask your two boys in the closet."

Lowe looked from me to Lu and back again. "So, then. Who are you? I doubt you're a researcher and a worried papa."

"On TV," I said pleasantly, "they would call me a hitman. And my lovely friend here used to be in the same business."

Finally I'd gotten through to him. The tan seemed to fade away as a paleness took over, all the blood draining from his handsome, hooded-eyed, trimly bearded face.

"Might I explain?" he said quietly.

"You can try."

The smug, smart-ass quality in his voice replaced itself with quiet sincerity. "I have a reputation—as you surely must know, having sniffed around town for the last two days—as something of a lady's man."

What a quaint old expression.

Our host waved a hand again, making another design of smoke. "I have dated many women, even while I was married, and I have admittedly avant-garde appetites that run counter to the typical mores of a town the size of, and as conservative as, Port City. So naturally certain suspicions have been raised, in the wake of these tragic, horrific murders of attractive young women. In particular this is due to my having known one of them—she worked at Lowe Trucking as summer help. But because of my reputation, which I admit is deserved, I make it a practice...forgive the crudity...not to defecate where I dine. My company has a strict non-fraternization policy, by which I abide and expect all of my employees to honor. But the young woman having worked for Lowe Trucking was enough to make me, as the authorities put it, 'a person of interest' in the investigation into these murders."

I said, "Did you speak to my daughter?"

The eyes weren't hooded now. "Your...daughter? She really is...your daughter?"

"That's right. It's not part of a cover story. I *am* Susan Breedlove's father. I know that she came to Port City to look into the killings, and you are a natural to be on her list of interview subjects."

He stabbed his cigarette out in a silver deco tray. "I, uh, did speak to her. Briefly at my office. Told her what little I know."

I leaned forward; the nine mil in my hand came up. "If you have her, and she hasn't been harmed in any way, I might let you live."

Might.

Lowe held his hands up, palms out, chest level. "Why would *I* have her?"

"Why would you sic that Keep on Truckin' pair on me? On *us*?"

The raised hands slapped the air. "Why else? I wanted to discourage you. Frighten you. Send you packing! A journalist and a concerned parent show up and start asking everyone and his dog questions—you've stirred up the police, and next will come publicity….You make this wrongheaded assumption that I'm guilty because, what? I'm the rare man who likes pretty young girls?"

"Are they?" Lu asked. "Pretty young?"

He stiffened. "I am no cradle robber, no pedophile. Just a small-town Lothario, with the means to at least try to rattle your cages and send you scurrying. That I freely admit. And it's all there is to it."

"Is it?" I asked. "If that's the case, why haven't you cooperated with the local police?"

That seemed to offend him. "Why, I've cooperated in every way, every respect!"

I lifted my left forefinger. "Except one—you've declined to be swabbed for DNA."

His chin came up. "I felt it was an invasion of privacy."

"Sure."

He folded his silk-sleeved arms and leaned back. "*But*… when Deputy Chief Maynard came around, to investigate the crime *you* committed—breaking and entering, here at my home? He asked me again about submitting to a DNA test… and this time? This time I allowed it."

Lu and I exchanged quick looks.

Lowe gestured sweepingly. "The chief swabbed me right here in this room. Said he intended to put a rush order in…and, thanks to the notorious nature of 'The Cheerleader Murders,' within a couple of weeks I should be entirely cleared….I know I don't have to show you the way out." He rose confidently to his feet. "You *did* know the way in, after all."

Rather awkwardly, Lu and I rose, the weapons in our hands held limply downward.

Then Lowe was reaching for the phone on his desk. "No, I'm not calling the police. I need to get a doctor in here to deal with Juan. I stand behind my employees."

✾

We returned to the Best Western Inn. Having decided that relocating was the better part of valor, we checked out. I asked the young bright-eyed desk clerk, possibly on uppers, if he could recommend an out-of-the-way bed and breakfast. He could and called ahead for us.

A few miles off the Highway 61 Bypass, on Tipton Road, Strawberry Fields was a big, rambling refurbished Victorian farmhouse as red as its name. The immaculate bed and breakfast was set well back from the highway on tree-spotted grounds with the light snowfall making an idyllic Christmas card out of it.

Our host—white-haired, middle-aged, in wireframe glasses and a light blue shirt with a Strawberry Fields logo—put us in the Berry Room. The vintage furniture there sported geometric designs and elaborate hardware, as if not quite knowing whether to be modern or antique. With exposed rafters, pale yellow walls and a patchwork quilt on the antique iron double bed, the Berry Room made for a cozy getaway—and its first-floor position with generous windows onto the lawn would make for a not-so-cozy getaway, should that prove necessary.

I stripped to my skivvies and got under the covers. Lu—in see-through skimpy bra and panties, which kept few secrets—sat on the bed next to me.

"This is romantic as fuck," she said with a smile. "I still have that nurse's uniform. Wanna play doctor?"

"I don't think so," I said, returning her smile weakly. "I'm just a little too distracted. I heard all that prick Lowe's excuses, but he still has an S & M dungeon in his basement."

She shrugged. "Everybody needs a hobby."

My jaw tightened. "Even if he didn't snatch Susan, I wouldn't mind killing that creep on general principles."

Her eyebrows rose. "Even though his innocence is probable after cooperating with Maynard on a DNA swab?"

I sighed. I seemed to be doing that a lot. "Yeah. I'm just frustrated."

A sympathetic nod. "And worried for your little girl."

"She was *never* my little girl. I didn't know her till she got to be a big girl, and I can't say I really know her all that well, even now."

"So maybe let her fend for herself, then? Or if she's dead, shrug it off? You know how we used to look at it. Somebody targeted for a hit is already dead. We just put the period on the sentence."

"You want out?"

"Goddamnit, Quarry. Will you please quit insulting me? Move over."

THIRTEEN

We were among a handful of guests at Strawberry Fields, and the owner/manager volunteered that this was one of his slowest times.

"Picks up on New Year's Eve," our host said, "for one-night overnight stays."

The other two couples staying here had already eaten their breakfasts in the small, beautifully appointed dining room, complete with tablecloth and china and Yuletide-ish floral centerpiece. The walls were eggshell white and a bay window with a holiday wreath still hanging let plenty of sunshine filter in through sheer curtains.

"The week between Christmas and New Year's," he said, in cheerful resignation, pouring Lu coffee (I had tea), "is no gift to us."

Henry Nelson, our host, with his wispy white hair and wire-frame glasses, looked a little like an elf that got laid off by that bastard Santa. Again in a light blue shirt with the B&B's logo, he was jolly and sad all at once. We'd already learned that he and his wife had taken on this business after years in real estate, seeking an idyllic semi-retirement. The setting certainly fit that description, the Victorian farmhouse strawberry-red among century-old oak trees on expansive grounds, a wooden gazebo and a red-brick barn bookending the main structure. But his wife had died of cancer two years ago and she was just a friendly ghost here now, her decorating choices pleasantly haunting the place.

"How did you like the French toast and scrambled eggs?"

Nelson asked, hovering with his coffeepot. "And those home-made cinnamon rolls?"

"Wonderful," Lu said.

"I'll second that," I said.

The old boy beamed. "My daughter does all the cooking. Emma's putting college off a few years to run the place with me."

Emma could be seen in the kitchen, bent down filling a dishwasher, a pleasantly plump redhead in an Xmas-red apron over green slacks and white blouse. She gave us a smile that thought it hid her weariness and got back to work.

Strawberry Fields served its breakfast in shifts, even when under-booked. So Lu and I were alone as our food was brought to us. Nelson hadn't been talkative at first, and we kind of forgot his presence, though we were at least somewhat discreet in our conversation.

"The names of the parents of the dead girls," Lu said, "were among Susan's materials. But no phone numbers or other contact info."

I said, "We might be able to get that from Deputy Chief Maynard."

She sipped coffee. "He's certainly been the most helpful of the local law enforcement types. But after talking to the parents, assuming we can arrange meetings with them, I don't know where we go from there."

"You assume," I said, "the parents will even *want* to talk to a true-crime researcher."

Lu raised a forefinger. "A true-crime researcher whose famous employer is among the missing, remember. Accompanied by the M.I.A. author's concerned papa."

In retrospect, that all might have sounded a little arch, and an eavesdropper might have sensed that we weren't either of those things, researcher or father—just pretenders with some unknown agenda.

But after breakfast, when we were having a last round of coffee and tea, Nelson appeared there between us, leaning in somewhat over the table.

"I apologize for listening in," he said. "I don't mean to be a snoop."

Neither of us found anything to say.

"Might I sit down?" our host asked, gesturing to an empty chair at the end of the table. Lu and I were facing each other.

"It's your house," I said. Neither friendly nor hostile, and my suspicion not showing. I hoped.

"It's these Cheerleader Murders, isn't it," he said, more statement than question.

"Yes," Lu said. "I'm researching the crimes for an author who's dropped out of sight since she hired me. This is the author's father."

Nelson looked from her face to mine. "You're talking about that Breedlove woman who drove down here from Davenport a time or two. Word gets around. Do I understand you're hoping to talk to the parents of these unfortunate children?"

I suppose to any parent, nineteen- and twenty-year-old girls are still children. And likely always will be.

Lu said, "Yes, we intend to approach them, but respectfully. We know the grief they're suffering is unimaginable."

He squinted, nodded. "Did I...forgive me...hear you say you needed contact information?"

"Yes," we both said.

"My late wife knew all of these gals, the mothers, I mean. They were in the PTA together, over the years. Bake sales, fall festival and so on. Would you like me to arrange something for you? Something here at the Fields? A soothing setting like this might, well, take the edge off."

Our host had developed scheduling skills, between breakfast shifts and event planning; and in about fifteen minutes he had lined up individual interviews with the mothers of the three murdered young women.

"I know it sounds trite to say so," said Laura Taylor, a grade-schoolteacher in her early forties, slim in a black cashmere sweater and pink blouse and dark slacks, "but Ashley was a good girl. Good student, good daughter, genuinely good person."

The Colonial-theme common room represented the oldest part of the farmhouse—vintage framed prints, fieldstone lighted fireplace, exposed beams, pine flooring, and comfy furnishings, including the two easy chairs we'd pulled around opposite the first victim's mother, seated on a cloth-covered couch.

The woman, her hair up and mingling black and gray, was sitting with her hands folded in her lap.

"Ashley dated the same boy through all of high school," she said. "Billy Reynolds. They were engaged. He died in Afghanistan."

Ashley's mother had chiseled cheekbones but the features they framed were strictly soft-focus—her eyes big and sky blue, her nose delicate, her lips thinner than they'd been in her prime though still lovely.

Her daughter must have been stunning.

"Ash never really got over losing Billy," the dead girl's mother said. Her dignity was impressive but brittle. "Just like she never got over losing her father when she was in junior high. He was fifteen years older than me. Massive heart attack. Smoker, I'm afraid. I never remarried, by the way. Work took the time, and the need."

I asked, "Where was Ashley employed?" The *"at the time of her death"* was understood.

"A waitress job at the Merrill. That's the new, nice hotel on the riverfront, five-star. Ash was saving up for college. Had her eye on Northwestern after community college. I could have afforded a state school, but she had other plans. Dreams, hopes, of acting. She'd been in plays since she was a little girl, and, of course, she was a cheerleader. Her team won all sorts of competitions."

Lu said, gently, "Going into acting isn't a terribly realistic pursuit. Even for a talented girl."

Her eyes flared, the thin lips formed a quick smile. "Oh, I know, and we had that discussion many a time. And despite that goal, my girl had her head on straight. She was minoring in education. If New York theater wasn't interested, she was prepared to teach her craft in a school somewhere. Just being around theater in some fashion was very important to her."

"Ashley dated the same boy," Lu said, "all through high school, you say. But what about after? Anything serious or even not so serious?"

Laura Taylor sighed. Her fist clutched a hanky but she didn't use it, her eyes swimming with tears that refused to fall.

"I wish I knew," she said. "We'd been so close, so very, very close, after her father died. It's funny. She was a daddy's girl and we had always been…this sounds so silly, even stupid… competitive."

Two beauties in one house. Not unusual.

"But after Russ died," the girl's mother went on, "Ash was mine. My friend. My rock, as was I hers. She shared every secret. This went on for years. Then Billy died overseas and she withdrew. She still lived at home, and we were pleasant to each other. You'd almost call it friendly. But that closeness…it was gone. I made a mistake."

Lu cocked her head. "A mistake?"

"Yes. When Billy joined up, went off to war, as they say…I encouraged Ash to start dating others. She took great offense. Poor judgment on my part."

I said, "So you wouldn't know if Ashley was dating anyone in particular toward, uh, the end?"

"No. She went out frequently...toward the end, as you put it. But never a word about with whom. And any query on my part was ignored. Ash was very secretive. Very protective of her privacy."

Sarah Edwards was on the heavyset side but handled it well, her black tailored suit and white silk blouse befitting her position as a legal secretary. Her face was round but very pretty, nicely framed by a medium-length blonde hairdo, and that her daughter Rebecca had been a stunning young woman came as no surprise.

"Becky was one of five girls," her mother said, "the middle child, but she lacked the insecurity some middle kids feel, that sense of not belonging. Her father was away, on the road much of the time, and wasn't close to any of his kids. Becky took the younger girls under her wing. And she did have that typical middle-child mediator gene. All her sisters loved her dearly. They still do. And I love her dearly."

With great dignity, she daubed her eyes with a tissue.

"I have nothing negative to share about my child," Sarah Edwards said, "not out of any sense of being protective, mind you. But she was a good, generous girl. Sometimes a bit...*too* generous."

"Oh?" Lu said. "How so?"

"You've seen a photo of her?"

I said, "Yes," not specifying that the young woman had been dead at the time, decked out in a sexy teddy, splayed in the snow.

Finely plucked eyebrows rose. "When people think of a cheerleader, the cliché? Becky was the kind of girl they imagine— sexy, shapely, blonde, a little giddy. She was not an outstanding student, C-plus at best. But she had a bubbly thing about her that, with those looks, made her popular."

"She was working," I said, "at Lowe Trucking."

"Just a summer job, post-high-school graduation. Becky was enrolled at Port City Community College. That's where she was attending at the time of her...passing."

Lu said, "In what way was she too generous?"

The woman's mouth twitched; her eyes avoided our gaze. "Becky was something of a wild child. An *all-American* wild child, but...let's just say that I got her on birth control pills when she was still in middle school."

That explained some of her popularity, anyway.

"But Becky was just too peppy, too *up*," her mother was saying, "for anybody to hold that against her. Sometimes girls who are...my parents used to call it 'fast'...are looked down upon. Becky never had a reputation as...oh I hate this word...a 'slut.' Just a girl who liked a good time. Liked it a little too much. Her junior year of high school, we had to put her in rehab."

"For drugs?" Lu asked.

"For alcohol. Becky was running with a crowd that was wild, even for her. When she graduated from rehab with flying colors, I encouraged her to go out for cheerleading. I knew that would require her to be physically fit and would put the beer parties on hold...at least during football and basketball seasons. It worked. She never had trouble in that regard again."

I said, "We appreciate your frankness, Mrs. Edwards. I can assure you I'll do my best to keep everything you've shared out of my daughter's account of the case."

The eyebrows went up again. "Please don't! I want Becky's story told. It's a...what is the phrase? A cautionary tale....Is there anything else I can tell you?"

I asked, "Do you know if your daughter was seeing anyone at the time of her passing?"

Nodding, she said, "I believe she was. Becky knew I did not approve of her promiscuous ways. So she kept that side of her life to herself. I do think...this is just an impression, though it does come from observation...that she may have been seeing an older man—not someone in her age group or, frankly, modest social class."

Lu leaned forward. "You say there's something you observed that made you come to this conclusion?"

One definite nod. "Yes. On the weekends, you'd have thought it was prom."

"Prom?"

"She was dressed to the nines when she went out. No one picked her up at home, by the way. Becky always took her car and met whoever it was. Do you think that's who killed her?"

I nodded. "Yes."

She shook her head slow and a single tear trickled. "How could anyone do such an ugly thing to a beautiful young girl?"

I said, "There are a lot of bad people in the world, Mrs. Edwards."

Stephanie Dawson, whose daughter Kayla was the victim who'd been found naked in the snow, could not have been thinner and still be alive. You could tell she'd been pretty once, but you really had to look past the sunken cheeks and absence of makeup, and her short white hair just didn't give a damn.

Though her daughter's death had occurred only weeks before, the only possible sign of sorrow might be her charcoal pants suit; but her silk blouse was a peach color that had nothing to do with mourning.

"Kayla lived for cheerleading," the Dawson woman said, in a

soft, dignified voice. She worked as head librarian at the Port City Library and earned the permanent whisper honestly.

"She quite excelled at it," Lu said, "we're told."

"I never really understood that, but it was very, very important to her. She was chubby as a child, then shot up and filled out in middle school, which is where she began her cheerleading obsession. I wasn't against it, of course, though the appeal eluded me. But it got her physically fit, on the one hand, and excited about something that wasn't boy bands on the other."

Lu asked, "Did Kayla get along with her father?"

"We rarely saw him. Earl and I divorced shortly after Kayla was born...she has one older sister, Lynn. This may sound strange, and I don't mean to be cruel or judgmental, but I have never had much interest in men. I had a certain physicality that attracted them, back in the day...but it always rather irritated and even...sickened me."

Lu asked, "Did your daughter share that view?"

Her smile was unexpected. "Oh, no. Kayla dated enthusiastically from thirteen until...until she was no longer with us. We weren't close, but she assured me from time to time that she was not...*overly* generous with her charms. It's difficult for a child who was once an overweight girl not to appreciate the new attention she receives when she's become a beauty. But there's an element of resentment, as well."

"How so?" I asked.

The girl's mother might have been talking about a lab rat. "An overweight girl who is suddenly shapely...like a short boy who springs up...always retains their former self within. So that...and forgive the armchair psychology...a formerly plump girl or tiny boy have a sense that only their new, superficial selves are attracting the opposite sex...or the same sex, in such cases. And if their real self was known by a suitor, they feel they would be rejected just as before. And are probably not wrong."

No tears from this woman. Not even a clutched tissue.

Her eyes turned from Lu to me and back again. "Is there anything else I can tell you?"

I said, "Was Kayla seeing anyone in particular in the weeks preceding her death?"

A bony shrug. "Not that I know of. Again, we tended not to talk of such things."

"No one came to pick her up at your home?"

The librarian shook her head. "No. Kayla took her car and met this individual elsewhere."

Lu said, "Then she was seeing someone in particular after all."

"Looking back at it, I would say yes. But I haven't the slightest idea who."

Lu asked, "Did Kayla dress up went she went out?"

"Yes. Like a little whore."

We took coffee in the elegant compact dining room, me at the head of the table and Lu at my right, and discussed what we'd learned from the three women: which is to say, not much.

"It does seem to point to an older man," Lu said.

"And a wealthy one. So have we circled back around to Christopher Lowe again?"

"Maybe."

"Look at it this way: at some point, just like the girls who got in Ted Bundy's car to help out a nice guy, these young women were approached by an older man...someone outside their age range but someone they felt they could trust...who then groomed them for sexual purposes. Whoever this is may have done this with any number of other girls, disposing of only the ones that presented him with a pregnancy problem."

Lu said, thoughtfully, "And all of these girls were short a father in their lives."

"And not just Kayla Dawson may have been on the make for a rich husband—Rebecca Edwards had been on the pill back in middle school, her mother said, but got pregnant after graduation."

Suddenly, as if materializing, Henry Nelson's daughter was there with a coffeepot, refilling Lu's cup.

Hovering, Emma looked toward the doorless archway into the living room area, dominated by an array of knickknacks, cabinets and shelving. Her father was at the front desk, registering a middle-aged couple, chatting them up.

"My father doesn't need to hear this," Emma said in a near whisper, and took the seat at my left, placing the coffeepot aside on the table. "I've heard snippets of what you've been talking about, with Pop and with those three friends of Mom's. I apologize for eavesdropping. But I know who the man is, the one that Kayla was seeing."

We just looked at her.

"Kayla Dawson was my best friend," Emma said.

FOURTEEN

Emma Nelson, seated to my right across from Lu at the oval table, leaned in to say, sotto voce, "It just *has* to be Chris Lowe."

Sun was streaming in through the gauzy curtains in a dining room that so typified the quaint bed and breakfast's nostalgic unreality. It was the kind of place that had you longing for a time that never really existed—like the statement the young woman had made that she'd seemed to immediately retract.

"You don't *know* that it's Lowe?" I asked her, annoyed.

The attractive redhead—her green-eyed good looks somehow enhanced by a baby-fat pudginess, a few random flying strands of hair lending a note of hysteria—glanced toward her father in the adjacent room, at his counter making nice with a couple checking in.

"Daddy doesn't want any trouble," she said. "These 'Cheerleader Murders' are bad for business, and so is having me out there spreading 'gossip' about one of Port City's leading citizens."

It hadn't stopped him from lining up the three mothers of the dead girls for us to interview. But there was a difference between getting these crimes cleared up and being out there rumormongering about them. Not that I really thought that was what Emma Nelson was doing. She had tears in her eyes and a tremor in her voice that said this was something else.

Lu said, "Christopher Lowe certainly qualifies as one of Port City's leading citizens. But why are you convinced he's the man Kayla was secretly seeing?"

Emma folded her hands, which were contradictions—work-worn but her fingernails touched with pink pastel polish. "You have to understand about Kayla. She had a certain shrewdness, but probably no better than average intelligence. She viewed her looks as her best asset....You've seen her picture?"

Lu and I nodded; we'd seen her photograph, all right. Of course, Kayla hadn't been at her best, sprawled dead in the snow, clad only in the nakedness she'd worn on her entrance into the world.

"You might say Kayla kind of dated with an eye on the future," Emma said. "She always had her sights set on the boys from good families...wealthy families....They were her...objective, let's say."

Lu asked, "How did she go about that?"

Emma swallowed. She produced a handful of tissues from under her apron. "Everybody knew Kayla put out. But everybody also knew she didn't put out for just *anyone.*"

"Let me guess," Lu said with a knowing smile. "She got handed around from one rich kid to another."

Emma frowned. "That makes it sound worse than it was. She'd go with one for a while, then move on, sometimes to greener pastures."

Money green, it sounded like.

"Hey," Emma said, with a weak smile, "Kayla was fun, had a really good sense of humor. Of course, not many of the girls liked her at Port City High—they considered her a boyfriend stealer. But I liked her. I knew she had a good heart, and that she was just trying to, you know, better herself using the physical means available to her. By our senior year, though, she'd become kind of a joke. Everybody saw through her. I guess I felt sorry for her."

"And you think she left school-age boys behind," I said, "and went after a new prize—Christopher Lowe. A wealthy older man."

Raising one eyebrow, Lu said to me, "Not *that* old—Lowe's only in his late thirties, you know."

"That's plenty old," Emma said, "when you die at nineteen like Kayla."

She wept in a tissue for a while.

Then Lu leaned forward. "Emma, I realize Kayla was your friend. But it does sound like she was on the prowl for something better. Someone richer."

Her face still damp with tears, the young woman nonetheless laughed. "That's the irony."

"What is?"

She opened a palm. "Look, Kayla never told me who this guy was, just that he was really loaded. Rolling in it! Only she wound up falling for the guy. He wasn't just a…means to an end. A ticket to a cushy life. She said he was really charming, and passionate. Thoughtful, caring."

Fifty Shades of Chris Lowe.

Emma was saying, "Kayla said they would go for rides in his cruiser on the Mississippi. They sometimes drove up to Galena for overnight getaways. And always, always romantic walks at Wild Cat Den."

One of the murder sites.

"She did say, kind of giggling about it, that he was into kinky sex. Such as what, I asked? But she wouldn't go into detail. Just fun harmless stuff, she said. It just went to show how sophisticated he was for someone in a little hick town."

Fifty Shades Darker….

"I told the police," Emma went on, "I suspected Lowe. That he fit everything Kayla ever mentioned about her nameless lover. How she thought she was stalking him, with an eye on the altar. But, really, *he* was stalking *her*."

I was thinking Emma was right about that when Lu said, "I don't think so."

"Oh?" Emma's eyes, dry now, opened wide.

Eyes Wide Open, I thought.

Lu waggled a forefinger. "Not stalking her. Using her, and when she wound up pregnant, he dumped her, dead, in that 'romantic' park."

Emma swallowed.

I said, "You say you've spoken to the police."

"Yes. I shared my suspicions, my opinions, with Deputy Chief Maynard and the sheriff. A detective from Davenport, too. I don't know whether any of them took any of what I said seriously."

"I'm sure they did," I said. When you're grasping for straws, you take everything seriously.

"I wish I had more for you," Emma said.

"You've helped," I said.

"Definitely helped," Lu said.

A little.

"There *is* someone else you can talk to," Emma said. "A reporter with the *Port City Journal.* Will Fisher. He's written a few pieces for both the paper here and their sister paper in the Quad Cities, the *Times*? He spoke with your daughter, or anyway Ms. Breedlove said she was on her way to interview him."

"She did?"

Emma nodded. "I spoke with her, too. She talked to Daddy and me, separately. She's pretty, and nice."

Lu and I exchanged glances again.

I asked, "What did you discuss with her?"

She shrugged. "Everything we talked about just now."

That meant there was no doubt that Susan had learned

Christopher Lowe was a suspect in the Cheerleader Murders, even if the police she'd spoken to about the case had been less than forthcoming.

Emma's father was in the doorless doorway connecting the dining room and the living-room/lobby. He gave his daughter an unhappy look, and she excused herself and went back to her kitchen duties.

Nelson came over and leaned in by the chair she'd vacated. "I don't know anything more than Emma does. Probably less."

I said, "You don't mind that she talked to us?"

"No. But I'd just as soon she didn't know that I don't. She's been obsessing over this thing and it's not healthy. I don't even know why that little round-heeled Kayla, rest in peace, means so much to her. And I know these suspicions she has about Chris Lowe have to be taken with a grain of salt."

"Oh?"

He nodded. Like his daughter, he near-whispered, as she was at work in the next room. "Emma had a couple of dates with him, not long after high school graduation—he spoke there …on 'Making a Difference.' You see, Kayla kind of swooped in and took Chris Lowe. She was a boy-stealing little bitch, that one—if you'll excuse the language, ma'am. But sometimes a harsh word is the only thing that'll say it."

In our room, we packed up and went over what we'd learned from Emma. And her father.

"So she was hedging," I said. "Emma does know Chris Lowe was who Kayla was seeing. Her best friend stole him from her."

Lu shrugged a single shoulder. "It's not a new story."

"But why lie to us about it?"

"Maybe she wants to help without getting in the middle."

That did make sense.

"I have to wonder," I said, "if Emma doesn't know first-hand about romantic boat rides and overnight trips and walks at Wild Cat Den."

The almond eyes widened. "And maybe spent a little time in that basement dungeon?"

I had no answer for that.

When we checked out, a few minutes later, we asked our host if he could provide the address of the *Journal*.

"No problem," he said, adjusting the wire-frames. "It's a bit of a haunted house, though."

We didn't ask him what he meant and he didn't offer it up.

The big red-brick two-story rectangular building with its time-worn gray-stone facade—several wings expanding it to accommodate printing press and loading docks—dated to 1919 (according to its cornerstone), and remained an impressive piece of work. Even its three central awnings were fashioned from stone, and above them were large letters spelling out

THE PORT CITY
JOURNAL

as chiseled to perfection by an artisan of another time with a forgotten skill set. Mark Twain, or anyway Sam Clemens, had been on the staff of the paper in the mid-1800s, extolling the sunsets over the Mississippi. Ellis Parker Butler had written *Pigs Is Pigs* in Port City. And I had unintentionally researched my first book here.

The entrance to the pressroom was around the corner on Cedar Street. This was an extension of the building, more red brick but likely dating to the 1970s. Lu and I went right in, though an out-of-use buzzer implied security had been tighter in earlier days.

I expected a bustling newsroom, but I was wrong. This was an area the size of a grade-school gym, its flooring well-worn green-and-white linoleum tile, the panels of its drop ceiling yellowed here and there like a bed-wetting child's mattress; the ghosts of wire service tickers could be made out and a counter across the way was piled not with news copy but assorted building materials. More ghosts indicated where perhaps a dozen desks had lived, an aisle between two rows of six. Only one desk remained, in the center of the room directly under a fluorescent lighting panel.

Looking like a refugee from a road-company production of *The Front Page*, the one-man pressroom didn't even look up from his computer keyboard as he batted out copy that appeared on the screen as if willed there. He was alone—so alone he was able to smoke with nobody complaining, a squat figure with a rumpled shirt and rumpled trousers and a rumpled face with a knob nose and beady eyes behind browline glasses.

He was typing so fast you could barely clock it, his brown hair so wispy you could watch it thin further.

"Help you?" he asked, without looking at either of us.

Two chairs stood alongside his desk, on the Cedar Street side of the building.

Before settling into them, I said, "This is Lila Anderson. She's Susan Breedlove's researcher. And I'm Susan's father, Jack Jamison."

He wheeled away from his computer and faced us.

"Okay," he said. "You don't mind if I smoke, do you?" His cigarette bobbling between rather thick lips seemed to give assent, so we didn't bother. "Unless you folks have an issue."

"All alone?" I asked. "What about out front? What about the printing press and loading docks?"

"No, just me, and not me at all after the first of the year. This building is up for sale and the whole *Journal* operation, except at the moment for yours truly, is being handled in Davenport, at the *Times*. How is Ms. Breedlove? She was a very pleasant little gal. Corker of a cutie, if you don't mind my saying."

"She's missing."

The eyes behind the lenses of the browline glasses woke up. "Missing you say?" He grabbed a spiral notebook and pencil off the desk, which otherwise was populated by a landline phone, a pack of Chesterfields, and several empty paper coffee cups; a vending machine was also present, off to our left, humming along—it didn't know the words.

Pencil poised, he said, "What are the circumstances?"

I raised gentle palms. "Let's not get ahead of ourselves, Mr. Fisher. You are Mr. Fisher, aren't you?"

"I am indeed," he said.

He was old enough to say "indeed"—probably past retirement, but I had an idea an editor realized this museum piece was worth keeping around, in case somebody needed to know how to write.

"So," the reporter said, "what's become of Ms. Breedlove?"

Lu said, "We're not entirely sure. She isn't answering her cell, and she isn't home." She glanced at me and I nodded permission. "Actually, her house had been searched, and not in an orderly way. Ransacked is how I'd put it."

His rumpled face swung toward me. "You suspect foul play?"

"Not out of the question," I said. "Let's not write anything down just yet, okay?"

"Okay. Not just yet. The police know?"

"They do," I said. "We haven't filed a missing persons report. Not yet. It's not been a week."

Though it felt like a year had passed since the killer calling himself Duval had come calling.

"There could be a hell of a story here," Fisher said. "You'll excuse my lack of sensitivity. I know you're concerned for your daughter's welfare. But I assume you're aware of what story your girl is working on?"

Susan was a "girl" to him, too. She wouldn't mind. Past forty, being called a girl doesn't seem so bad to some women.

"Well aware," I said. "We're conducting a kind of unofficial investigation ourselves into the Cheerleader Murder case."

"Hell of a title." He grinned and it was strictly yellow journalism. "Make a whale of a TV movie. I could retire on that puppy. Don't mean to downplay what you're going through, of course, wondering if your kid's okay."

"Of course."

He glanced around at his shabby fluorescent world. "That's why I'm still here. I was supposed to be gone two months ago. Retired the hell out. Kids are grown, wife passed three, no, four years back. I got nothing better to do than pound these keys. But it's gotten to be kind of rote…and then these headline murders come along. Again, forgive me. I always figured tact was something you put on the teacher's chair."

"Then," I said, "you're here because they want somebody on the ground in Port City should something break."

He gestured with the pencil. "That's right, and to do local interviews and color and such. You know, I view your daughter as my competition, in a way."

"Why's that?"

He cocked his head. "Like I said, there's a hell of a book in this. Cheerleaders, that's sex. Serial killing, that's violence. And sex and violence is what makes the world go round. What sells papers. What makes for a juicy true-crime story. I'll sell it to TV or maybe the movies, and spend the rest of my days on a beach in Florida finding some woman younger than me who wants to live the Good Life and is willing to let me have my way with her, once a week or so, and maybe pop the pimples on my back now and then."

"Everybody needs a dream," I said.

Lu said, "Susan Breedlove is a name author, though. She has a brand."

Fisher waved that off. "No question. But if she turns up in, uh, a bad way? That clears the path for me, and I do apologize for such a cold fucking way of looking at it. If she writes a best-seller, hell, I'm the guy like you said, on the ground, who saw all the sex and violence up close and personal. She gets the *New York Times* and my knockoff paperback gets the airports. Everybody wins."

Goddamn airports again.

"Okay, Mr. Fisher," I said. "You're a relic with a wish. So am I, and my wish is to find my daughter alive and well because I have reason to believe your Cheerleader killer took her. And I intend to pop a cap in his ass."

Lu was shocked by my frankness.

But all Fisher did was look at me with steady (if rheumy) eyes behind those lenses. "Where do I know you from?"

"...Nowhere."

The eyes narrowed. "You been around here before. Long time ago."

"No, my first time in your little jewel of a city."

"I read that book you wrote."

"I didn't write any book."

"I think you did. I read a couple of those. You like to make yourself look good, don't you?"

"Not *that* good."

He grinned at me.

I grinned at him.

"Here's the deal," I said. "Tell me everything you know and I'll talk to my daughter about adding you to the byline of *The Cheerleader Murders*."

"You'd do that?"

"I would. You'd have to pull your weight. Do whatever writing is called for, whatever research."

He stuck out a grizzled hand. "Sign this contract."

I shook his hand. "Now. What can you tell me I don't already know?"

Most of what he had, however, came directly in line with what we already had from Emma and the cops.

I was just about to give up on this effort when he said, "I can tell you're disappointed in what I have to offer."

"No," I lied, "you're doing fine."

His sigh was a cigarette-ravaged thing that seemed to rattle his lungs. "Pity they made that park ranger a part-time gig."

"Why is that?"

He shrugged. "Well, you could've talked to him out at that little shack. He'd likely be able to confirm seeing Christopher Lowe and that Kayla child together out there, walking paths and such. You'd have Lowe and the girl directly linked. Which would be helpful as hell, 'cause Lowe has otherwise been pretty discreet. His policy is pay his wenches off, or—if I'm right about him—kill them off."

Lu was sitting forward. "The ranger's part-time, you say? So he isn't out at the Den?"

"No, they shut that down during the winter."

I asked, "Is he on call, this ranger?"

He gave us that Yellow Kid grin. "Not hardly. He's no fool. He winters down South. That lucky bastard's *already* kicking back in Florida."

In the Lexus, behind the wheel again but not starting the

vehicle up, I said, "She's dead, isn't she? Why would this prick Lowe, or whoever is responsible, keep her alive?"

She touched my coat sleeve. "It's not been that long, Quarry. Maybe they still hope to make her talk about what information she might've shared with somebody."

"Shit." I hit the steering wheel with the heel of my palm. "She's gonna turn up dead in some fucking park, isn't she?"

"Maybe not. In a park, possibly…but maybe not dead."

FIFTEEN

Mid-afternoon, with me at the wheel this time, Lu and I took Highway 22 from Port City, following the river into rolling countryside. Below us, hugging the shoreline, were flood-defying cottages, often on stilts, while at above left mansions with magnificent river views kept their distance high on bluffs.

Ten miles and a few left turns later we found ourselves in Wild Cat Den, a surprising eruption of forest and rock that put the lie to the notion that Iowa was just one cornfield after another. The park's eclectic terrain and staggering views were catnip for campers; but that was in summer with its pine-shaded trails and autumn with its coats of many colors. This was winter, when trees were skeletal and waterfalls silent and sandstone cliffs foreboding, where sun-reflecting greenery was replaced by shades of brown and gray.

You could not call our presence anything but a hunch. Anything else would be a lie or an exaggeration. But one of the girls had been dumped here dead, as if she weren't cold enough already, and with that park ranger's shack empty, what better place to keep a hostage? The Cheerleader madman never re-peated a dumping ground. Any official investigation in this wilderness of seventy-foot cliffs and centuries old pines was long since over.

We parked the Lexus in the otherwise empty lot on the park's east side, got out of the vehicle and gave the area a slow scan. Tourist attractions included a nineteenth-century grist mill and a one-room schoolhouse, not that any tourists had been attracted on this cold, gray day.

Then we took stock of our weapons—my nine mil and Lu's .38 revolver, with a spare mag in my bomber jacket pocket and a moon clip in her black puffer pocket. That black topcoat she'd inherited from dead Duval was too cumbersome for this purpose. She'd bought the waist-length jacket at the Port City Mall, and the moon clip too, when we'd made a stop to buy hiking boots.

Locked and loaded, we crossed Wild Cat Den Road to the central trail. Snowfall this December had been relatively light so far, and brown dirt pockmarked the thin layer of white. We started out, surprised by how rapidly the landscape rose, a steepness that warned hikers what lay ahead, with tall bare trees on either side of a path about ten feet wide like the central aisle of a cathedral, but one that had burned to its scorched columns and was then abandoned by its builders.

Could this really be Iowa? Through the barren trees and the touches of stubborn green, you could see sandstone and limestone bluffs towering like surrealistic statuary. At an early intersection with another trail, wood-burned signs pointed to such colorful spots as Devil's Punch Bowl and Horseshoe Bend (to the left) and Steamboat Rock and Fat Man's Squeeze (to the right). Occasionally we passed a camp area with a fire ring and picnic table, small grassy clearings frosted irregularly white.

Breaths smoking, we followed the winding trail to the left along the rust-and-tan face of a cliff, a nearby creek, not yet frozen, burbling over rocks and branches. Our pathway was a mixture of dirt and rock and occasional patches of grass with snow sprinkled like a baker's powdered sugar. The trail's natural flow took in steep climbs and assorted terrain, rocky bluffs soaring nearby. Surrounded by the austere beauty of rock outcropping, sandstone precipices, and bottomless ravines, I could only wonder if we'd walked past where Kayla Dawson had slept on the snow with a towering pine as her grave marker.

And a thought made me shiver more than the cold: would we come upon Susan's frozen form laid out just the same?

The trail took us over several wooden bridges, whose creaking objections were the only sounds other than wind in the trees, the stirring of branches and the ruffle of remaining leaves; on each bridge we hung onto the railing with our left hands, our right hands in our coat pockets, clutching the guns. We were moving through a chill, eerie, almost silent world. No songbirds, no rustle of brush, no animal cries. Perhaps the park was in mourning.

Or maybe the intrusion of invaders off-season, like the ones that had disrupted my quiet life up north, had silenced them.

Finally we came to another clearing, at the foot of a rise that flattened into the modest plateau of a yellow-tan cliff. Like the camping areas, the browning grass was sprinkled white, and at its center sat what had to be the ranger shack, a fairly pathetic representation of Man in the midst of all this Nature.

The rustic ranger station probably dated to the 1930s days of the Civilian Conservation Corps. An outhouse, fire ring and picnic table were nearby, sad signs of relative civilization. The gabled, one-and-a-half-story house had a timber-framed porch and wore ancient brown shingles as siding like the scales of some long-extinct beast. The windows had green shutters, recalling the Lowe mansion, though the paint here was blistered.

The shutters were shut.

Revolver in hand, Lu waited on the open porch while I circled the shack, looking for signs of recent use. The latest layer of snow obscured any footprints. Woods surrounded two-thirds of the small clearing, the approach to the cabin dependent on the trail and the rise of the nearby cliff. I listened to the silence, but it wasn't really silence at all—the rush of the creek we'd passed whispered and an owl had something to say. The usual question. Its answer came from a crow's caw. Not very instructive.

I joined her. "Nothing. Nobody. Let's have a look inside."

The front door, new compared to the building it protected, was locked. I had brought my lockpick packet, but I was impatient and kicked it open instead. Took three kicks, but I didn't mind: I had frustration to work out.

The interior had been redone a few decades ago, which made it seem comparatively modern. We were in a shallow outer area that, with its cheap tan vertical paneling, might have been a motel check-in desk suitable for an unfussy adulterer: a counter with Indian arrow plaques in front (National Park Service, U.S. Forest Service Rangers); shabby chairs with split vinyl seat cushions (green—this was nature, after all); and a rack of color brochures of attractions and accommodations in the area (the only thing here dating to the twenty-first century).

Lu watched the door while the nine mil and I went around behind the counter into a stubby hallway. At right was an empty little room, door standing open, with a beat-up metal desk. Another small room had a table, possibly for food prep. No bathroom, no sign of running water. Well, they had an outhouse, didn't they? What other amenities could you need?

On the other side of the short corridor were two doors, one closed, the other standing open, and here at last were signs of life: a pile of firewood, bedding, a lantern, a flashlight, dishes and cookware, matches, toilet paper, first-aid supplies, trash bags, dish soap, towels and an ice chest. These were piled here and there, vaguely organized into groups. The accumulation suggested occasional occupancy—someone was here not all the time but enough to want such creature comforts handy as toilet paper and matches.

That left a door.

I pressed my ear to the wood. Nothing. I jiggled the knob. Locked.

"*Susan! Are you in there? It's your father!*"

From within came a muffled wail, a human voice expressing distress and hope and despair and relief all at once.

"*Lu!* I think she's in here."

This door took only one kick; perhaps it was original to the ancient shack or maybe I was just motivated. But at any rate it flew off its hinges and slapped the wood-plank floor as if trying to bring it to its senses.

Susan lay splayed on a bare mattress on a green painted metal bed frame, its headboard against the wall opposite as I rushed in, Lu lingering in the doorway. This was a private family moment, after all. My daughter's big blue eyes were goggling at me, her blonde hair askew; but with that silver slash of duct tape over her mouth, her expression might have conveyed joy, fear, happiness or any combination thereof. Her wrists were attached to the headboard, in surrender mode, by police-grade steel handcuffs, and two larger cuffs were around her ankles, securing her to the metal foot of the old bed. Her legs spread apart like that was unsettling enough, but she had been dressed (by whom?) in a generic cheerleader's uniform, short red skirt and white crop top with USA on it in blue letters.

This seemed to answer the musical question: how does a serial killer known for murdering cheerleaders outdo himself after leaving his last victim naked?

"It's all right now, honey," I said.

Lu was poised in the doorway as I gently removed the duct tape and, freed, Susan's mouth said, softly, "Daddy."

She sounded so young saying that, this woman of forty or so, who had only called me "Daddy" once before and then it had been teasingly. But this was a sincere, heartfelt, eyes-moist delivery that should have all of you reading this going, "*Awwwww!*"

Me, I was just thinking how somebody was going to die, at

my hands, but without my usual dispassion. Revenge a dish best served cold? My ass.

Like any good former Boy Scout in the forest, I was prepared. In my lockpick pouch was a handcuff shim designed to open standard pairs of ratcheted handcuffs. One at a time, I slid the shim between the pawl and the ratchet and quickly released each cuff. It took maybe a minute and a half and felt like an hour.

Still sitting on the bed, Susan threw her arms around me and hugged, really hugged. First time for that, too. I hugged back the same way. Also a first.

I asked, "Who did this?"

"He…he always wore a mask," she said, voice trembling, her usual confidence nowhere in sight. Still on the edge of the bed, she rubbed her wrists. "One of those…bondage masks? Black, rubber or latex or something. For the first…first two days I was in some kind of S & M chamber. Maybe…maybe a basement."

I helped her onto her bare feet. Lu looked around and found some trainers that seemed to have been Susan's.

Susan was looking into recent memories and they weren't pretty. "He wanted me to…to eat dog food from a dish. I told him to go fuck himself. He told me I'd be begging for dog food before this…this was done. And you know what, Jack?"

I was Jack again. The short sweet life of Daddy.

"What, sweetheart?"

"I would *kill* for a dish of dog food right now. I haven't had a bite to eat or a drink of water in six days."

"I think we can do better than that. We'll hit a drive-through."

That made her laugh. It was a bit hysterical, but a laugh, and I forced a smile and said, "We should get the hell out of here. I'll give you my jacket."

I stuck my nine mil in my waistband and was climbing out of

the jacket when I heard Lu cry out and the man with a gun at her throat, holding her from behind in the doorway, said, "Hands up, Mr. Jamison. And stand away from the girl."

Deputy Chief Maynard was ducking down behind Lu, a trained cop like him knowing not to give me an angle on the kind of head shot that would shut his motor reflexes off like a switch; and with my gun in my waistband, he'd have plenty of time to shoot me before I got to it.

Even with Lu in front of him like a shield, her expression apologetic, I could tell the big burly, sandy-haired, trimly bearded cop was in full regalia, a black leather police jacket unzipped to reveal the dark blue, badged uniform underneath. No wonder the investigation, the thrown-together unofficial task force, had never gotten anywhere.

I did as I'd been told, edging away from Susan, my hands up. He was not here to explain, he was not here to talk at all, but to either round us up and herd us into a squad car and take us off somewhere and kill us; or just start shooting now.

And the latter seemed his favored option, because his arm snaked past the captive Lu's head, the snout of a Colt Python revolver zeroing in on me like he was shooting paper targets on a police firing range.

That was when Lu bit him on the right hand, hard, blood dripping like his flesh was crying, and he howled and fired the weapon, its boom shaking the small bedroom, but the bullet going past me to thunk into the drywall. He didn't drop the gun, which with his bleeding, bitten hand took some doing; but he was surprised and off-balance and when Lu elbowed him in the stomach and wriggled out of his grasp, he knew he was fucked.

He was gone from that doorway in an instant and then I was in pursuit, saying to Lu, "Stay with her!" Probably a needless thing to say, but you know how protective fathers are. I had my

nine mil ready and was running down the short hall just as he
was pushing through the door in the outer room and heading
outside, on the run.

Not wanting to give him a target, I dove out the open door
and rolled, and his bullets flew over me, whip cracks in the air.
He had two choices for routes of retreat—the trail we'd come
on to backtrack, or the rise to the cliff's plateau, which would
present another way out with a steep but navigable downhill
path. He chose the second option—perhaps it was the better
path to his squad car.

Maynard was younger than me, at least twenty years, and he
was bigger, taller, heavier; but that wasn't strictly muscle he
was carrying around. He was huffing and puffing as he ran and
I was prepared to blow his fucking house down, me, Quarry, an
old man who swam every day and had kept the weight off.

I had not been much of a father—hell, I hadn't been a father
at all, really, except biologically. But I would be goddamned if
this prick with a badge, this predator playing protector, was
going to get away with what he'd done to my daughter, and
what he'd almost done to her. No fucking way.

He stopped, halfway up the incline, breathing hard, and
tossed a couple shots back at me, the whip cracks echoing, but
I hit the deck and rolled this way and that, damn near going
over both times, yet he missed. He fucking missed.

I wasn't running any faster than before, but he was going
slower now, he was tiring, and then I was on him, tackling him,
taking him down on that plateau, an area not much larger than
a wrestling mat. The sweet part is that my tackle sent his gun
flying. The bitter part is my nine mil flew out of reach, too. I
could see it, but I couldn't concentrate on retrieving it without
giving him the advantage.

And now, goddamnit, he did have the advantage. Suddenly I

was the dog that caught the car. He was big and heavy and strong and maybe fifty and I was past seventy and he was on top of me, and not in a friendly way, though in a sense he was preparing to fuck me, all right. I was on my back at the edge of the cliff, never a good place to be unless you're the hero of a 1940s serial. I was protecting my face with my forearms from what seemed like ham-size fists, and so he worked on my stomach instead. I tensed up, all that swimming coming in handy; but that only went so far. I had to stop protecting myself and swing at him again, unleash those powerful fists of mine that for some reason were bouncing off him like poorly made snowballs.

Then his hands were on my throat and squeezing and my world was going red and then black and just before I confirmed my suspicions about the afterlife, a gunshot split the silence—a gunshot punching the air, crack and fade, then again, crack and fade.

And Port City's Deputy Chief of Police reared back and looked at what must have been a hell of a view before I rolled to one side and I swear what I saw next was Susan with Maynard's revolver in her sweet hands, standing there on the plateau in her trainers with Lu just behind her. Then my little girl did a fantastically timed cheerleader's kick in Maynard's ass and he went flying.

Right off the edge, and he wasn't dead yet, though I made out the red dot in his back as he went windmilling down, preceded by ribboning blood as if he'd just crossed the finish line, and when he hit, the sound seemed more like an echo, a thud, dull and unimpressive and distant.

But it had made an impression, all right.

Seventy-five feet down, Maynard was making a snow angel, but soon it became a static one; not entirely static, because blood flowed for a while, surrounding him with a scarlet Rorschach ink blot. Not that it would take a trip to a shrink to learn this guy had been psycho.

I stood looking down at him and said, "Rah yay sis boom bah, motherfucker."

Cheerleader Susan was next to me. "Who are you supposed to be? Bruce Willis or Arnold Schwarzenegger?"

"Well, I am an '80s kind of hero, don't you think?"

And she hugged me again.

Then she looked over at Lu, who was retrieving my nine mil from the snow.

"Nice of you to drop by, Jack," my daughter said, then nodded at Lu. "Who's your friend?"

"Oh, we go way back," I said.

I gave Susan my coat and she walked on my left and Lu on my right as we went back down.

"You must be one proud papa," Lu said.

"I knew just how to raise her right," I said.

SIXTEEN

At the green-shuttered mansion overlooking the river, up the black wrought-iron half-stairway to the stoop, I rang the doorbell. The night sky had decided to stop being gray and was now a brilliant dark blue with a chunk of moon and more stars than you could count.

I was alone. Lu and Susan and I had made a couple of stops since our visit to Wild Cat Den—to buy a few functional clothes at Wal-Mart for Susan and to re-register at Strawberry Fields so we could all clean up and rest a little. I got into a fresh sweatshirt and jeans, put the nine mil in its shoulder holster under my left arm, slipped the fur-collared bomber jacket on and went off to call on Christopher Lowe.

He didn't answer right away, but he did answer. The tanning-bed bronzed man with the short black hair in a Caesar cut was again in that maroon dressing gown with the black lapels and cuffs. And slippers. A skimpily bearded man of leisure. Wealth and leisure.

At first he just cracked the door a bit, thought for a moment, before widening it some.

"Do we really have anything to talk about, Jamison?" he asked. His tone was dismissive—he didn't have high enough an opinion of me to be contemptuous. "I already admitted sending those truckers around. If you want to pursue it legally, that's up to you. But I have friends on the police department."

"Past history," I said, waving it off. "I need your help. Or, anyway, could use your advice. In this instance, I frankly didn't know where else to turn."

His grin was sudden and white against the tanned flesh and dark beard. "You must really be desperate."

"I am at that. May I come in? Could we talk for a few minutes?"

He mulled that. His handsome Hugh Grant-ish features turned momentarily ugly, in a flash of scowl, then he sighed and let me in. I closed the door behind me.

"You'll be relieved to know," I said, "that my daughter has been found alive and well. Unfed for six days, but not beaten or otherwise abused."

His expression turned benign. "Well, that *is* a relief. I trust she's cleared me of the suspicions you held in that regard."

"She has. I have a feeling you'll be astounded when you learn who *was* responsible." I gestured past him. "Is there…somewhere we could sit and talk? I have a lot to fill you in on."

"Certainly." His manner had shifted into something almost friendly. Civil, at least.

Again he led me down a hall and into the dark wood and mahogany study with its walls of shelved leather-bound, unread books. He settled on the brown-leather couch and I pulled up a chair with a comfortably padded backrest and seat cushion. As before.

I told him how I'd found Susan being kept hostage in the park ranger's shack at Wild Cat Den. Told him about Deputy Chief Maynard showing up and threatening us—Lu and Susan and I—with a weapon. Told him how Lu, held by him from behind, had bitten the man's hand and how he'd fled, and how I'd pursued. The whole story, including that Maynard had gone over the edge and taken a long, fatal fall. I implied that I was responsible, though, and did not include Susan sending the chief to his doom with a cheerleader kick in the ass.

"Jesus," Lowe said, the tanned face going pale. "When *was* all this?"

"A few hours ago. After six days, Susan needed a bite to eat, a chance to bathe and clean up, and a little moral support. You can imagine."

He rolled his eyes. "Actually, I can't. What that poor girl seems to've been put through is literally unimaginable. What an incredible encounter with this lunatic. You've reported the incident to the police, I assume?"

"I have not," I said. "That's why I'm here."

He shifted a little on the couch. "Frankly, while I'm pleased to hear that your daughter is safe, I don't see how this has anything to do with me. Other than it will finally clear up the suspicions that some people around town have stupidly held about me in these terrible crimes. When you have a little money, people just love to think the worst of you."

I nodded. "Yes, that lifts a burden off your shoulders. In retrospect, it makes sense that Deputy Chief Maynard was the perpetrator in all of this. He fits the profile, so common in serial killer cases, of someone these young women would trust. You can easily imagine him luring any one of these girls into his police car for a ride home or on an imaginary family emergency of theirs. In what would seem an innocent or helpful gesture."

Lowe folded his arms. "Still, you obviously have to report this. The longer you wait, Mr. Jamison, the worse it might go for you."

"I'm well aware of that. And that's one of the reasons why I thought to come to you first. You're a respected member of the community, a local captain of industry."

"That may overstate it."

"I don't think so," I said. "Add to that your familiarity with Port City, as a lifelong resident, and your knowledge of the way its political machinations grind."

"I don't follow you."

I opened a hand. "It's simple. How can I go to the police and report this, when Maynard was one of theirs? How can I know how interwoven his actions might have been with accomplices on the force? Susan believes two people were involved, after all."

"*What* other person?"

I grunted a non-laugh. "She doesn't know. He was masked— one of those black bondage things, made out of latex, with eye and mouth holes. But the build of this second individual was different, less husky, more slender, somewhat taller than Maynard. There was never more than one of them at a time with her, but she's convinced two men were involved. Could be any number of others on the Port City PD."

He nodded slowly, thoughtfully. "You could go to the sheriff. Or to that detective in Davenport. They're both actively investigating these so-called Cheerleader Murders."

"Yes, with Maynard. How do I know one of them isn't this other masked man? It's not the fucking Lone Ranger. And have you forgotten that I have my own skeletons in the closet? I would not like to have to stand up to a thorough investigation."

Lowe shrugged, shook his head. "So where do I come in?"

I leaned forward, hands folded. "You must be tied in with people in local politics that you trust. The mayor, perhaps. Is the chief of police someone you place confidence in? Look, Mr. Lowe, these are the waters you regularly swim in. I'm just a stranger in town, with a checkered past. Help me out here."

Does it sound like I was vamping? Stalling for time?

That's because I was.

I'd left the front door ajar for Susan and Lu to be able to enter and search the basement apartment of our unknowing host while I kept him busy. And I was just running out of gas when Susan burst in, holding something draped in her hands...

...something black and shiny and damn near liquid.

She flopped the flimsy garment next to him on the couch and he goggled first at her and then at it, at what might have been the hide peeled off a madman, and in a sense it was: the hooded black latex bondage body suit she'd seen one of her two captors wearing, the shed skin of a human snake.

I will give him this: he reacted quickly, as if he'd been living his life on the permanent edge of exposure, ready to bolt at a second's notice, which is what he did—he flew off the couch, before I was even barely out of the chair, and as he moved through he straight-armed Susan to the floor as if he were a running back, rushing past her, a racehorse coming from behind for a surprise victory, astonishingly fast for a guy in a robe and slippers.

I helped my daughter up and we quickly followed him as he predictably headed for his front door, but he froze when he saw Lu standing there blocking it, with the shattered alarm box still unrepaired to one side of her. She had the .22 she'd confiscated from the late Duval in her gloved hand, clad in the black jump-suit, but she didn't fire because Susan and I were coming up behind him.

Lowe cut right, to a doorway tucked under the second-floor stairs. Lu and I knew from our prior search of the place that this led to the occupant's basement apartment, and then he was gone and we were all looking at each other with frustration and dismay. We'd planned this carefully and yet he'd slipped out of our grasp anyway. We should have known it wouldn't be this easy. After all, we were literally on his home ground.

We trailed after him down the narrow unlighted stairs with me in the lead and the two females pressing me to move faster than I would allow. The basement apartment had enough illumination to create an unwelcoming glow at the bottom of the dark stairway. Emerging from there, we would potentially be sitting ducks. Again, this was his turf and Lowe could be waiting with a weapon—a gun, a knife or some implement from his kitchenette, even just a chair, anything to slash or bash us with if a firearm weren't handy.

That meant creeping down cautiously and when we neared the doorless aperture at the bottom, I turned to the women and pointed to myself, then pointed toward the apartment, and held a hand up to them, stop fashion. I hoped they understood I meant to go in first and they were to follow only after we knew where Lowe had positioned himself.

I dove in, my nine mil in hand, and rolled and bumped up against one end of the pool table centered mid-room, then ducked around behind it.

No gunshot, no tossed object or swung chair had greeted me. And he had nothing to hide behind, the leopard-spread bed headboard flush to the wall, the flat screen TV mounted, the mini-kitchen open to the rest of the room. From the walls, football imagery stared us down on one side, bikini women grinning at us from posters on the other like fake-breasted banshees.

As I peeked around the edge of the pool table, I saw why no defense had greeted us: the door onto the patio facing the river stood open, a storm door swinging like an effeminate slap. He'd made his escape, apparently.

I waved the women in.

They came out of the stairwell quick, staying low, Lu in the lead with the .22 in hand, Susan with a revolver we'd provided. I held up a hand indicating they should maintain their positions and I went to that open door, put my back to the wall alongside the opening, grabbed a deep breath and dove through, pushing past the swinging storm door. If I were alive tomorrow, I would pay for all this expenditure of energy, senior citizen that I was; but my brain was in a much younger mode.

Pitching forward, I rolled, anticipating being greeted by some nasty response—gunfire maybe—but all I heard was wind whispering in the trees and a tugboat horn on the river below, blowing me a raspberry. I was on the patio's fieldstone tile, sitting there, where I'd come out of the roll, like a kid playing jacks. The moon and stars wondered what the hell I was up to. So did I.

I perked my ears, thinking Lowe might have gone around to his freestanding garage; but no garage door was going up or car roaring away. I got to my feet and crossed the patio, empty of furniture this time of year. There were concrete block stairs going down to the river but no sign of him, with the landscaping such that he had nothing much to hide behind.

With a pissed-off sigh, I headed back inside. I didn't have to wait till tomorrow to pay for all this exertion; I was scraped here and there and my muscles and bones weren't happy. At all.

In the basement apartment, I looked at the two women standing in front of the pool table, and I shrugged.

Then my eyes landed on the closed door to the owner's playroom. His little S & M dungeon. I curled a finger and Lu and Susan trailed after me. I tried the door. Locked, of course.

What else? I got my lockpick packet out to again open the Yale lock. Stood to one side as much as possible as I performed the task, which slowed me some. Took me thirty seconds that seemed a lot longer, because who knew when bullets might come flying through that door? I made sure Lu and Susan were standing off to either side. Once I had the door unlocked, we didn't go immediately in, instead we all instinctively moved away, still in the outer room, in case bullets might punch through at us. The fake-titted bikini babes looked on in leering derision.

But no bullets came.

I reached my hand around, searching for a light switch, and found it quickly, flipped it on. The little red-walled, black-ceilinged dungeon was underlit, but you could make it all out, the stocks, spanking bench, drop-down chains, hand-crank suspension hoist, the six-drawer black metal cabinet of fiendish toys, all the sick goodies a homebody fiend might desire, including of course, against the wall opposite the entry, that big black wooden X. The dog dish had apparently been washed and put away. No guest present to dine from it.

And in the far left corner was our host.

Christopher Lowe was sitting pressed against the join of red cement block walls with his legs up and clutching them to him, his eyes big and terrified; he was trembling like the frightened immature boy he was. His slippered feet made him somehow pathetic, the silk robe, too, like a hospital patient that had wandered into a nightmarish operating room. The chamber had, after all, finally realized its objective: creating abject fear...although in this case, it wasn't the victim, or even a willing masochist, who was the recipient, but the sadist who'd designed it.

"Give me a hand," I said to Lu.

As soon as she figured out what I was after, she helped me cuff him to the X. He did not protest. He seemed catatonic. Or perhaps just defeated, resigned to his fate—a monster the townspeople with torches had finally cornered.

We stepped back and admired our handiwork.

Susan, behind us, only a few feet inside the dank room, was looking on in quiet horror.

The Cheerleader Murderer hung there like an evil Christ, every limb as loose as a stringless puppet's, eyes in the tanning-bed-tanned face staring past and through us and everything

else here. Perhaps he knew that every evil fucked-up thing he'd
done had finally caught up with him.

Lu, next to me, said, "What do you have in mind, exactly?
Are you going to leave him hanging there, to starve to death?"

I waved that off. "Ah, somebody'll hear him down here, when
he comes out of his funk and starts in screaming. And everything he's done will come out…except, with any luck, our part
in it."

Susan said, quietly, "Nobody will hear him. This room is
probably soundproofed."

Lu shrugged. "Maybe that nice cousin of his will find him."

"Or not," I said.

SEVENTEEN

We decided to spend New Year's at Susan's place in Davenport. It just made sense. Since my daughter hadn't been declared officially missing, she was able to tell Davenport's Detective Reeves that she'd merely taken a few days off and her researcher and father got unnecessarily worried.

As for Lu and me, we answered whatever questions we were asked—Sheriff Sloat talked to us, too, and the Port City police chief—and we were able to do so with surprising honesty... mostly because nobody knew the right questions to ask.

While it hadn't made the papers yet, Reeves said it looked like a resolution was on the horizon for the Cheerleader Murders. Seemed after Christopher Lowe went missing for nearly a week, his cousin had discovered him half-starved and in a state of dehydration in what would be described by the *Quad City Times* as "a nightmarish sado-masochistic hidden playroom."

Though the investigation was ongoing, the president of Lowe Trucking was now the prime suspect, currently hospitalized having suffered a severe psychic break. A belated DNA swab—Maynard had submitted one earlier, from some unknown party—tied Lowe to all three murders.

"Probably cop a fucking insanity plea," Reeves bitched.

Well, in fairness, he *was* insane.

Early in the new year, some hikers found Deputy Chief Maynard's body and his fall was initially written off as a tragic accident, a terrible way for such a respected civil servant to meet an end. A bachelor with no family, he'd given his all to protect and defend the public. Then when an unexplained bank account with a balance of several hundred thousand dollars came to light, it was suggested Maynard might have been a paid accomplice in the homicides—particularly when the ranger's station near where he plummeted seemed to have been used as a holding cell for victims. With Jason Lowe innocently providing movie-night alibis for his cousin, the Deputy Chief appeared to have committed the murders that Christopher planned, staged and arranged.

Susan's book on the Cheerleader Murders was mostly written but on hold until Lowe was either charged and convicted or committed to a mental institution; the latter would give her the ability to name him speculatively as the apparent killer. At my urging, she met with the *Port City Journal*'s Will Fisher and signed him on as a collaborator. Another airport bestseller seemed destined.

My book, I assured her, would change the names and be wildly fanciful. She was fine with that.

We all had a little too much to drink bringing in the new year. Champagne, of course, but nothing pricey. Susan made lasagna and we didn't stick our noses out that night. It didn't get as dangerous out in the wild as it used to. Aggressive DUI's had lessened that risk. Still, why tempt fate?

I think my daughter and I were a little embarrassed by our behavior—me acting like an actual concerned father, rescuing her; and us both going all soppy sentimental. But I do think it brought Susan and me a little closer. Lemonade from lemons.

"You got into the father game a little late," Susan said, as I helped her in the kitchen.

"Guilty as charged."

"You made up for it."

That was nice to hear.

Lu and I figured we shouldn't hang around too long. Why

give the authorities any more time than they deserved? They might just get ambitious. We shared the driving and spoke little. We were comfortable together and it was nice to just be traveling without an agenda. No car locks to pick, no sub rosa hospital calls, no house break-ins.

We got back to Sylvan Lake around five P.M. after a long day of driving, and wound up at the 371 Diner in Brainerd. I don't recall what we ate, but the conversation lingers.

"Listen," Lu said. "Sometime, when you've got nothing to do, why don't you come visit me in Billings?"

"Montana? What, and punch cows?"

"I'm serious."

I shook my head. "I wouldn't want to put you at risk."

The almond eyes bore in; her lips split the difference between smirk and smile. "Nobody knows you there. And I'm somebody else, since I died. Who can say what'll develop?"

There it was.

I waited to deal with it till we were back at my place, sitting on the couch taking in the warmth of the fireplace, which was snapping, crackling, popping, like the old kids' cereal.

"Getting back together," I said, "in a more permanent way... or as permanent as two older people can manage...is probably not a good idea. Occasional reunions, maybe. Anything more would only increase the risk of our pasts catching up with one or both of us. It's been nice to be together again and reminisce. I mean, we're good together."

Lu nodded. "We are. We understand each other. Two of a kind."

"Two of a kind." I slipped my arm around her, drew her closer. "Stay a day or two. Even off-season, there's good places to eat, and they aren't all pancake joints."

Her laugh was a throaty murmur. "Nothing wrong with pancakes."

"Of course," I said, "there's not a lot to do around here this time of year, I grant you. Let me ask you something."

"Yes?"

"You still have that nurse's uniform?"

QUARRY'S CODA

The previous novel in this series, *Quarry's Blood* (2022), was meant as a kind of coda to *The Last Quarry* (2006, written expressly for Hard Case Crime), which I'd intended to be the final entry chronologically. But the novel's unexpected success (unexpected by me at least) inspired a whole new run of Quarry novels at HCC, as well as a short film, a feature film, a graphic novel, and a Cinemax TV series (one season, but that counts).

Quarry's Blood reflects a story idea that required my semi-retired hitman to be closer to my age than the flashback novels (set in 1970s, '80s and '90s) had been. *The Last Quarry* already had been about an older version of the character—my age at that time. Later, HCC editor Charles Ardai convinced me to write a coda to my Nolan series by way of *Skim Deep* (2020), a ride I enjoyed taking. *Quarry's Blood* made a natural companion piece to that novel.

So at long last the Quarry novels had come to a conclusion!

And then *Quarry's Blood* was also more successful than I'd anticipated, racking up Best Paperback Novel nominations from the Mystery Writers of America ("Edgar") and the Private Eye Writers ("Shamus").

That seemed to signal writing another Quarry, and I had intended to write another flashback novel; but what I came up with had me writing about the older Quarry again, encouraged by the response to *Quarry's Blood*—writing a coda to the coda. *Quarry's Return* also has echoes of the first Quarry novel (*Quarry*, 1976, originally *The Broker*), although that book is not chronologically first. *The First Quarry* (2008) is.

Confused yet?

I find myself in my seventh decade revisiting my series characters Nolan, Quarry and Nathan Heller, compelled to age them with me. Quarry has always been a sort of left-handed autobiography, and of course most first-person novels have an autobiographical element, more or less.

My hunch is that if I revisit Quarry again (or maybe if he revisits me) it will be a flashback book.

My thanks to David Riggan, who gave my wife Barb and me a generous, gracious tour of TanTara Transportation Corporation's facilities on the Muscatine, Iowa island. Also, thank you to my editor Charles Ardai, who has allowed me to expand Quarry's world; agent Dominick Abel, whose friendship I treasure; and my lovely bride of fifty-some years, Barbara Collins. Barb's editorial acumen as my first reader is a major contribution to all of my work.

WANT MORE QUARRY?

1

I waited for her to come, and when she did, so did I. I asked her to lift and she lifted and let me get my hands out from under her. Here I'd been cupping that ass of hers, enjoying that fine ass of hers, and then we both came and suddenly her ass weighs a ton and all I can think about is getting my hands out from under before they get the fuck crushed.

I rolled off her.

"Was it good for you?" she asked.

"It was fine."

There was a moment of strained silence. She wanted me to ask, so I did: "How was it for you?"

"Fine," she said.

That taken care of, I got off the bed, slipped into my swim trunks, trudged into her kitchen, and got myself a bottle of Coke.

"Get some Kleenex for me," she called from the bedroom.

I was still in the kitchen. I said, "You want something to drink?"

"Please! Fix me a Seven and Seven, will you?"

Jesus, I thought. I put some Seagram's and Seven-Up and ice in a glass, got her some Kleenex from the bathroom, and went into the bedroom, where she took both from me, setting the glass on the nightstand, stuffing the Kleenex between her legs.

There was a balcony off the bedroom, through French doors, and I went out and looked down on the swimming pool below. It was mid-evening, and cool. Florida days are warm year round, they say, but the nights are on the chilly side, particularly a March one like this.

Not that the crowd of pleasure-seekers below seemed to mind.

Or notice. Lean tan young bodies, of either sex, their privates covered by a slash or two of cloth, basked in the flickering glow of the torch lamps surrounding the pool. Some of them lounged on towels and sun chairs as if the full moon, which I could see reflected in the shimmery green water of the pool, was going to add to their already berry-brown complexions. Others romped, running around the pool's edge or in the water splashing, perpetual twelve-year-olds seeking perpetual summer.

I watched one well-endowed young woman tire of playing water baby with a boyfriend, climb out of the pool, tugging casually at her flimsy top which had slipped down to reveal dark half-circles of nipple. She was laughing, tossing back a headful of wet dark blond hair, shoving at the brawny chest of the guy who was climbing out of the pool after her. He pretended to be overpowered by her nudge and waved his arms and made a show of falling back in, but she no longer seemed amused.

She wasn't beautiful, exactly. The girl in the bedroom behind me was more classically beautiful, with a perfect, high-cheekboned fashion model face and a slim but well-proportioned figure. A lot of the girls at this place (which was an apartment complex for so-called "swinging singles") were the model type; others were more All-American-style beauties, sunny-faced girls sung about in songs by the Beach Boys. She fit neither type.

Her face was rather long, her nose long and narrow, her eyes having an almost Oriental slant to them. Her mouth was wide and when she smiled, gums showed. Her figure was wrong, too: she was tall, at least an inch taller than my five ten, with much too lanky a frame for those huge breasts. Put that all together and she should have been a goddamn freak.

But she wasn't. The big breasts rode firm and high; she carried them well. Her face was unique-looking. You might say haunting. The eyes especially, which were dark blue with flecks of gold. Her voice was unusual, too—a rich baritone as deep as a man's, as deep as mine, in fact—but for some reason it only made her seem all the more feminine.

I didn't know her, but I knew who she was. I was here because of her. I'd been here, watching her, for almost a week now. If she noticed me, she gave no indication. Not that it mattered. The beard and mustache, once shaved off, would make me someone else; when we met in another context, one day soon, she'd have little chance of recognizing me, even if she had managed to pick me out of this crowd (which incidentally included several other beards and plenty of mustaches, despite the unspoken rule that tenants were to be on the clean-cut side in appearance, if not in behavior).

I hoped I wouldn't have to kill her. I probably would. But I hoped not. I wasn't crazy about killing a woman, only that wasn't the problem. I hadn't counted on her looking like this. Her picture had made her look almost homely. I'd had no idea she radiated this aura of some goddamn thing or another, some damn thing that made me want to know her, made me uncomfortable at the thought of having to kill her.

"Hey," she said.

I turned.

This one's name was Nancy. She was wearing a skimpy black bikini. She had short dark black hair and looked like a fashion model. Or did I mention that already?

"You want to go down and swim?" she asked.

"Later," I said.

"Is that Coke good?"

"It's fine."

"How come you don't drink anything but Coke and that? Got something against liquor?"

"No. I have a mixed drink sometimes."

"What d'you come out here for?"

"It's nice out here."

"Is it because you knew I'd smoke?"

"I guess."

"Don't you have a single fucking vice?"

"Not one."

"Tell me something."

"Okay."

"You always this blue after you do it?"

"Just sometimes."

"Every time. With me, anyway. You always get all, uh, what's a good word for it?"

"Quiet."

"No. Morose. That's the word I want."

"Quiet is what I get. Don't read anything into anything, Nancy."

"I knew a guy like you once. He always got... quiet... after doing it."

"Is that right."

"You know what he said once?"

"No."

"He said, 'Doing it is like Christmas: after all the presents are open, you can't remember what the fuss was all about.'" And she laughed, but it got caught in her throat.

"What are you depressed for?"

"I'm not depressed. Don't read anything into anything, Burt."

Burt is the name I was using here. I thought it sounded like a good swinging singles name.

"My husband used to get sad, sometimes, after we did it."

Him again. She talked about him all the time, her ex. About what a son of a bitch he was, mostly. He was an English professor at some eastern university, with rich parents who underwrote him. He (or rather they) paid for Nancy's apartment here in Florida. There was a kid, too, a daughter I think, living with Nancy's parents in Michigan.

"You know what he used to say?" she asked.

"Something about Christmas?"

"No. He used to say that in France coming is called the little death."

"That's a little over my head, Nancy."

"Well, he was an intellectual. The lousy prick. But I think what it means is when you come, it's like dying for a second, you're going out of this life into some place different. You're not thinking about money or your problems or anything. All you can think of is coming. And you aren't thinking about that, either. You're just coming."

Down by the pool, the girl I'd come here to watch was sitting along the edge, kicking at the water, while her blond boyfriend tried to kid her out of her mood.

Nancy's hand was on my shoulder. I looked at her and she was lifting her mouth up to me, which meant I was supposed to kiss her, and I did. I put my hand between her legs and nudged her with a finger.

"Bang," I said.

She took my arm and pulled me into the bedroom.